ONE WOLF
NEXT DOOR

EFTHALIA

Disclaimer:

One Wolf Next Door

By Efthalia

Copyright 2026

This is a work of fiction, created without use of AI technology.

This book contains mature themes and is only suitable for 18+ readers.

Contents

DEDICATION

TO ALL MY READERS -
THIS IS FOR YOU!

XOXO

Chapter One

Samantha Willow twitched her nose, raised her hand and spoke the spell, *huc*. A faint light zapped at the box of ribbons she'd been trying to reach. The box crashed to the floor, and a multitude of colors scattered in every direction. A puff of air escaped from her lips, blowing a few strands of hair out of her eyes. "I don't know why I bother."

She bent to collect the mess, and an ache started deep in her bones. She rolled her neck from side to side, tired of trying to get back into her coven. They had cast her out and kicked her to the curb for her shoddy magic.

Nobody. Wanted. Her.

Or her flawed incantations.

She was a bumbling ninny, and the magical world all knew it.

"You are an embarrassment to our coven." The words rang clear in her mind.

They simply didn't care for her because she was nothing and couldn't contribute a single decent spell to a community that only supported successful witches and warlocks.

She pushed the thoughts from her mind and placed the roses, lilies and magnolia foliage in circular formation. Her regular customer would be here any minute. Bewitching Blooms was right in the heart of town, and she had scraped every penny to make her dream a reality.

The sky had darkened, and rain pelted down. The bell over the door rang. "Good evening, Sam." Her regular customer dropped his umbrella in the bucket she had by the entrance.

"Good evening. I'm just finishing up your bouquet for you."

Mr. Rutherford bought flowers for his wife at the end of every week. Men like that didn't exist in the modern world today. Sam knew because she had lived in it for thirty defective-witchy years, and the regular flower buying guys were in their seventies.

A pang hit her square in the chest. What she would give for a lasting romance.

She did try to spell some hot guys, but each time her poor hocus-pocus skills backfired, and she ended up with burns or cuts to her skin. Images flashed in her mind of her hot neighbor with the dark brown hair, and his amazing abs just added to the whole package.

May her spying, witchy instincts be forgiven, she'd seen him taking out the garbage with nothing on but his shorts, and it was clear he worked out. A lot.

Mr. Rutherford cleared his throat. "Off with the pixies this evening?" He'd clearly picked up on her lack of focus.

"Something like that." She smiled while tying the ribbon, then held the bunch out to him.

"Thanks, Sam. You really have a way with flowers." He gave her his credit card.

"A lot of practice." She winked and handed him his card back when the transaction had cleared. "Have a good evening."

"You too, Sam. See you tomorrow."

A chill shot up her spine at his words. He came in weekly, not daily. She mustn't have heard him right. She gave herself a mental shake. She really should just clean up and head home.

She eyed the broom, twitched her nose and thrust out her hand so it could come to her. The broom shot through the shop, knocking over vases, pots, flowers and everything else. She ducked under the counter and waited for the rogue broom to drop. It did. Right next to her. A vase of flowers dropped on the counter, and water and flowers sloshed over the side and onto her head. "Really, should give up trying."

She got to her feet and looked around the shop. Her malfunctioning magic caused chaos. "Great, this is going to take ages to clean."

She picked up the culprit that had caused the mess. "Why couldn't you just come to me?" The broom tingled in her fingers. "Oh, now you hear me."

It tingled again.

She poked her tongue out at it and got to work.

Two hours later the mess she'd created with a simple twitch of her nose was finally cleaned. She exited the shop and popped the door open on her van. Sliding inside she let out a deep sigh. Maybe it was time to start living like a human with no powers. What was the point if she couldn't execute a proper spell? Tonight's failed attempts further proved she would never be able to harness power like other witches. "Time to throw it out the window, Sam," she whispered, veering the van onto the main road of town and heading toward her house.

Her thoughts drifted and became darker. No parents, no coven, nobody. She had nobody. She was a nobody. A thick tear slid down her cheek. She needed a change and a drink. Boy, did she need one of those.

She drove in the direction of the liquor store and jumped out in the rain to grab a bottle of gin. Then half soaked she dived back into her car. She was tempted to open it and start drinking, but drinking and driving were not a good combination. A minute later she pulled up in her driveway, pressed the button for the garage door to open and eased in.

She made her way to her kitchen and switched on the lights while peeling her wet t-shirt off and throwing it over a chair.

She looked out the window to see her hot neighbor peering in. His stare intensified and heated then a shit eating grin broke across his face. She squealed and ran for cover. "Shit, shit, shit."

She'd forgotten their kitchen windows looked into each other's, and she hadn't flipped the shutters closed for privacy. She raced to the living room where she had a pile of folded clothes, grabbed another t-shirt and threw it over her head.

"Really, Sam, you're such a moron sometimes."

The whole saga had left her feeling hot and bothered. She really did need to get out and date. Although the more she thought about it, she realized even that would be difficult. She was socially awkward, or at least she believed that of herself.

She made her way back to the kitchen and slowly moved to the window. She put her hand on the shutters and edged her head to one corner to peer out. Her neighbor was no longer in view, but that didn't deter her from snapping them shut.

She let out a sigh of relief and then went to the fridge to pull out some ingredients to throw together a quick dinner.

The doorbell rang and she jumped out of her skin. She made her way to the front door and pulled it open. Her pulse jumped up a few notches at the whole package of gorgeousness standing on her porch with her dog, Gilbert, in his hands. Guilt stabbed her in the chest. She hadn't even realized her faithful pooch wasn't in the house. She'd become so accustomed to him being curled up in her bed when she got home she didn't even think to call out. She bit her lip and her throat dried up.

"I thought you might want this little guy back."

His voice. It was the first time she'd spoken to him. She'd been meaning to go over and introduce herself but hadn't had the nerve.

Her voice box found the right sounds. "I'm so sorry. I don't know what to say. Gilbert rarely wanders away from the house."

"I found him at my back door." He held Gilbert out to her.

She reached for him, but Gilbert didn't want to move. *I wouldn't either,* she thought.

"I'm Dex." He held out his hand.

"Samantha, or just Sam." She shifted Gilbert to take Dex's hand. Her fingers closed around his big warm hand. It was a brief moment of contact, but power tingled around their closed hands. Heat fused its way up her arm, and his gaze bore into hers. She felt as naked as the day she was born. She dropped her hand and cleared her throat. "I'd invite you in, but I really do have to get to bed."

His lips turned up in a panty-melting grin. "Next time then."

"Sure." Good one, Sam. Sure what? That you'd invite him in or to bed. The latter sounded much better.

"Good night and keep an eye on Gilbert." He winked.

She watched him walk down the stairs then closed the door with a soft click and put Gilbert down. "What is wrong with you?" she scolded, and he took off running. "Silly thing."

She trotted back to the kitchen and fanned her warming cheeks with her hand. She felt hot all over and very bothered. Her neighbor Dex was the stuff of fantasies. She shook her head to get crazy images out of it.

"Get your head out of the gutter, Sam," she whispered to herself.

Gilbert came trotting back with his toy bear in his mouth. That was his language for bedtime. She bent down and gave him a few pats. "In a few minutes little guy."

He dropped the bear, barked, and then picked it up again before racing up the stairs. He'd be asleep at the bottom of her bed by the time she got up there. This was their routine. This was her norm—her every day.

She could hear the padding of Gilbert's paws upstairs and headed to the kitchen for sustenance. Reaching for a glass she moved to the fridge for ice and tossed some in her glass then poured in gin and tonic and added a slice of lime. She took a sip. "Just what the doctor ordered." She was too tired to make a decent dinner so opted for a quick sandwich. She ate it faster than expected then washed it down with the gin and tonic. Her thoughts had been bouncing around about the event she had to decorate tomorrow. She was only halfway through the table centers. She took a deep breath and filled her lungs and then let out a long breath of air. "Looks like it's going to be an early start."

She took the stairs two at a time and headed straight for the shower. The warm fuzzy feeling all over hadn't left. Was she this desperate for attention. She looked at herself in the mirror. Her long blonde mane looked decent given that she'd neglected her usual trim, but the evidence she was tired was definitely under her eyes.

Her shower was quick and once dry she threw on her t-shirt and a pair of underwear and took soft steps toward the comforting look of her bed.

She wiggled in and pulled the covers over her. Her eyes fluttered and she closed them, hoping she'd get some rest.

Sam stood in a room full of her coven's most powerful. They weren't pleased with her. The air crackled around her.

"You're an embarrassment to our community."

"Are you even sure you're a witch?"

"There's no place for you here."

"You'd be better off as a sideshow gimmick in the circus."

"Find another coven."

The insults were hurled one after another. Each one slashed through her with the precision of a surgeon's knife.

The lashings of her so-called coven of witches and warlocks were nasty. Nasty to their own kind for not being as talented.

Nasty because they saw her as defective. She had just lost both her parents and had no one to guide and protect her.

She cowered and pulled her hands up over her head for protection.

Beams of power swirled in their hands, and she knew exactly what they had in mind. She was going to be the subject of their attack.

Fight. A small voice from the dark recess of her mind said, *Fight.*

She straightened her back ramrod stiff as her anger rose. The ebb of power tickled her fingertips. She'd had enough. She would not let this group of bullies keep pestering her and mocking her for her erratic power.

She braced for the onslaught.

"Leave the child alone." A man stepped from the shadows.

"Why are you here?" one of the warlocks from her coven asked the stranger.

"To ensure you don't all overstep your boundaries. What you're doing here is overstepping the boundaries."

A few of the witches got to their feet and hurled power at the stranger. With a flick of his wrist, he turned their power back toward them.

Samantha's mouth dropped open. She was sure she was catching flies. How was that even possible?

She knew enough about magic to know you couldn't throw someone's power back at them. You could dissipate it and counter it in other ways, but she'd never seen a witch or warlock throw someone's spell back at them.

She scanned the room and the faces of her coven. Fear danced in their eyes, and their faces turned ashen.

"We don't want any trouble," one of the other witches said.

"The child must stay here until she's of age, but know this, if you hurl another blast of power toward her I'll know and I'll come for you all."

The stranger dematerialized from the spot.

Chapter Two

S amantha tossed and turned all night. The dream was always the same. She shifted again, trying to wipe it from her mind. She had better things to think of than that wretched coven she had grown up with, like her hot neighbor.

Oh yeah, Sam, *all that muscle*. Great, thinking of him didn't help; it made things worse. She started heating up.

"This is stupid." She pulled the covers back and headed to the shower. The more she envisaged her hot neighbor the more she wanted to go over to his house and ask for a cup of sugar or something more.

She turned the taps on, let the cold water blast her. She let out a scream, and Gilbert came running, barking continuously. "Calm down, it's just water."

He turned and trotted back out of the bathroom.

She had just enough time to soak her hair before a loud banging came from the front door. "Damn it."

She turned the taps off and grabbed a towel to dry off then threw a bathrobe on and bolted down the stairs to open the door. Her mouth dropped at all the hotness taking up the door space.

Dex was standing there in nothing but his pajama bottoms. She scanned his face, losing herself in those blue eyes before doing a slow crawl down the expanse of his chest to his toes. Holy mother in heaven this man was perfection. She'd never be able to wipe this moment from her consciousness. She shook her head when she realized she was ogling. When she locked eyes with Dex again, he was grinning.

"Like what you see?" His deep voice did nothing to help.

"Um, um. Why are you here?"

"I heard a scream." Gilbert came scurrying along and headed straight to Dex's feet. Dex bent to pick him up, and the traitor started licking his face and chest.

She was envious in that moment and cleared her throat. "Um, that was just the cold water."

"Do you have problems with your plumbing? I could take a look." He was still grinning, and there was a definite sparkle in his eyes.

Why did it feel like he wasn't really talking about her watering system? A wave of heat hit her. She needed to get him off her front porch before she threw him down and had her way with him. Images flashed in her mind—she naked with Dex. "Ah, no. It's all good. Just a little clumsiness on my part."

She made a move to grab Gilbert. "Thank you for checking in. Come on, Gilbert."

He wouldn't budge.

"Come on." Another tug. Something loosened from around her. She took a step back, but she wasn't fast enough. Cool air caressed her skin.

Dex's eyes widened and she knew she was on display. As brief as it may have been, it was enough time for her hot neighbor to get the lay of the land. Her clumsy hands grabbed the light material of her bathrobe and she tried to cover herself.

It was his turn to ogle. He licked his lips.

She fumbled with the strings. Finally she found the lapels of her robe and tightened them to conceal her body.

"Do you need help with that," he asked.

She swallowed hard. She needed a lot of things, but her reaction to her neighbor was unfounded and embarrassing. With a tug at her robe again, to make sure it was secure, she stuck her hands out for Gilbert, but the little traitor liked Dex's arms better. She wrapped her fingers around Gilbert and tugged, but this brought her into closer proximity with Dex.

He took a long inhale through his nose and moaned.

The sound tingled all the way down to her lady parts. She needed to get rid of him—now. Clearing her throat, she pulled Gilbert with all her strength from his arms and took a few steps back. "Thanks for coming to check on me. I think it's time I got ready for work."

"No problem." He took a step back.

She tried not to stare at the expanse of his wide chest, but her eyes traced their way downward.

He cleared his throat.

"Thanks again." She moved to close the door, and as soon as her neighbor was out of sight, she let out a deep breath. "You're trouble," she said to Gilbert. She bent to put him down and he scurried off. She made her way to the kitchen, then turned around and headed back upstairs to finish her shower. This time it would be a cold one. She needed to cool down. "Way to go, Samantha, flashing your neighbor."

She dropped her bathrobe and stepped into the shower, letting the cold water hit her. She didn't squeal. After a minute she altered the temperature to warm and pushed all her thoughts about her wicked, hot neighbor out of her head. The shower did the trick. She dried her blonde hair and applied light make up, then dressed in well fitted jeans, a loose shirt and threw on some comfortable shoes. When she was satisfied that she was ready for human consumption she headed to the kitchen for coffee.

She put a pod of coffee in her machine and waited for it to extract the elixir she craved. She opened her kitchen blinds and moved to the island bench to sit with said elixir in hand.

There was something calming about that first cup of coffee in the morning. To say Dex had rattled her ability to think straight was an understatement.

The sneak peeks she'd been having from her window didn't do the man justice. He was way, way hotter up close and in her personal space than what he appeared from the window or when she spied on him taking the garbage out.

She'd been meaning to go across and introduce herself but felt stupid, so it had been four weeks since he'd moved in and she'd never followed up on that promise. Yet her scream in the shower had brought him to her door. She wrapped her fingers around her cup again and brought the cup to her lips for another sip. *He's got some super hearing.* The thought danced around in her head. She dismissed it. "I've got good lungs, that's what it is," she said to Gilbert as he trotted over to her. He barked at her a few times. "Honestly, I swear you know exactly what I'm talking about some days."

Gilbert wagged his tail then turned and raced out of the room.

"That dog." The traitor had looked really comfortable in Dex's arms. She hated to admit she liked the look of him cuddling her dog. With the last sip of caffeine, she swung herself around from the stool she'd been sitting on. She glanced at the time and realized if she was to open her shop in time, she needed to boogie. Grabbing her keys and bag, she made her way to her van. She had flowers to collect from the suppliers before she headed to Bewitching Blooms.

Chapter Three

When the blue and red lights from the police cars caught her attention, the hackles at the back of her neck rose, and the closer she got, the deeper the dread seeped its slow path into the pit of her stomach, leaving a boulder.

She parked the car as near to her shop as possible. There was a lot of commotion, and an ambulance had just turned up. Her feet moved quickly but when she got near the shop the area had already been taped off. Someone was on the ground. Someone she knew. Someone who was her customer, Mr. Rutherford, and he wasn't moving.

She lifted the tape to approach, but her view was blocked by a hot tall muscly officer. She read his name tag.

"I need to get through." She pointed. "That's my shop, and that's Mr. Rutherford."

The officer's demeanor changed. "You need to come with me." He lifted the tape to let her through. "Over here," he indicated.

She caught sight of Mr. Rutherford. There was blood everywhere, and it appeared someone had stabbed him several times.

"Who would do something like this?"

"I need to ask you a few questions."

"Sure."

The hot officer flagged another police officer over. Only this one was in civilian clothes with a badge at his belt, and the way he moved made her breath hitch. She shook her head. She must be in heat or something because every male since her encounter with Dex this morning had her drooling. Either that or somehow she'd been blind to the men in her town.

"This is Detective Caspian Nicholls, and I'm Officer Eric Andor."

She stuck out her hand. "I'm Samantha Willow."

The detective and officer raised an eyebrow at the same time.

"How do you know the deceased?"

A chill ran through her, and she cleared her throat. "He's a customer."

"You own that florist shop."

"Yes."

"Why do you think he died in front of your shop?"

19

"Well, that's a stupid question. How would I know? He was a regular customer who picked up flowers for his wife every week. I saw him last night."

"Every week?" Officer Andor asked.

"Yes. Like clockwork."

"That's a lot of flowers."

"According to you but not to him. He was a sweet, old-fashioned man."

"Did he ever engage in conversation."

"Apart from the daily it's a beautiful or not so great day weather wise, no, just the usual weekly pleasantries."

"Did he show signs of stress or paranoia?"

"Stress, paranoia?" She repeated the words, shook her head and her gray matter caught on. "That man…" she pointed to the body "… walked in and out of my shop with a smile every week. He seemed like the guy with everything right in life."

"Well, Ms. Willow, appearances can be misleading."

"You don't say."

"When was the last time you saw him?"

"Yesterday, as I said."

"What time?"

"Same as every week. Four in the afternoon—sharp."

"Did he look distressed?"

She thought back to yesterday. "Not really. Same as any other week."

"In what way?"

"He came in, bought flowers. I rang it up and then he left." She shifted her weight to the other foot.

"Would you say he looked happy?"

"Yes, as I said. Same as always." Her conversation reminded her of Groundhog Day. It sounded like they were asking her the same questions only in a number of different ways.

The detective turned his gaze to Andor.

"I'll say it one more time, there was nothing unusual about his purchase." She let out a small huff of air. "If you don't mind, I need to get inside to start my day."

"We may need to ask you a few more questions."

"I'll be right there." She pointed to her shop and opened her mouth to say they were done.

"That's all. You can go."

She closed her mouth and dove into the safe haven of her shop. Inside she broke down in tears.

Who would do something like that to a nice old man, and why in front of her shop? And that policeman and detective? It seemed they were trying to implicate her in all of this. She'd never harm anyone. She just wasn't capable of it. With shaky hands she looked at the orders for the day. She'd need to go back out there where all the mayhem of police and reporters were to get fresh flowers. She looked out from the display window and several reporters were snapping photos of her shop. "Great, Sam. We're going to be on the news."

She'd work on the orders she could fill with stock she had in the cool room. She got stuck into it. An hour and a half later she finished her event flowers and completed three small orders.

The bell on the shop door rang.

She looked up to see Detective Nicholls and Police Officer Andor.

"We'd like you to come down to the station for further questioning," Detective Nicholls said.

"Why?"

"Maybe there's something you forgot or missed."

"I've told you everything I know."

"Perhaps."

"What does that mean? You think I would obstruct justice or something?" Why the no good, of all the things… if only her magic was normal, she'd zap his ass to Siberia.

"I never said that. I said maybe there's a small detail you missed."

"Like what? He came in for his weekly flowers and left." Her mind did a backpedal at her words and stopped.

"What?"

"I just remembered. When he walked out, he said see you tomorrow. I thought I misheard, but it was definitely tomorrow. He was a weekly customer. Why would he have said that? Could it have been a coincidence?"

"That's hard to say, maybe he was meeting someone here today."

She shook her head. "No, he was pretty much a walk in and pick up his order kind of man. He never hung around outside the shop."

"See, you did remember something with Detective Nicholls questioning."

"I did, but that's the whole story. There literally isn't anything else."

"That might be the case, I'll still need you to come down to the station and give a statement. It's procedure." The detective turned to head out.

"Fine. I'll get my orders done for the day then come on over."

Officer Andor lingered. "How much are those roses?"

"Oh, uh, thirty-five dollars."

"Can I have those delivered?"

"Yes, you can. Just give me a minute to grab my pen." She got the details and completed the transaction.

"What a way to start the day." She huffed.

"On that, we are all in agreement," Detective Nicholls said.

The bell on the door rang again.

It was one of the pesky reporters. "Ma'am, we'd like to ask you a few questions about the body outside."

Officer Andor turned to face them. "You won't be asking any questions. Back out of the shop."

"But..."

"*Out.*" He ushered them through the door. Then turned his head. "Lock the door, you're bound to get more in here when we clear out."

Great, just what she needed.

"Can you hang around until I get my van from out back. I need to unload more flowers?"

He nodded. "I'll stand at the front of the shop until you're done."

Samantha grabbed her keys and scurried around the counter. When she stepped outside, there were all manner of forensic people taking photos and picking up any bit of evidence they could. She ducked and weaved around everyone to get to her van. It was sheer dumb luck that no one parked behind her. Her quiet little street had turned into a nightmare. She reversed and brought her car around the back entrance of the shop. Then unloaded as quickly as she could, locked her van and entered through the back of the shop.

"Excuse me. Can we talk to you?"

She heard a voice and turned to see a reporter and cameraman walking in her direction. She bolted inside and slammed the door shut. She bolted the lock then pushed away from the door and headed to the front. True to his word, Officer Andor stood guard. She opened the door just a crack.

"Thank you. I've had a few around back."

"Don't worry, I'll clear them out."

"Thanks."

He winked at her.

She gave him a smile and locked the front door. She didn't know how long it would be before everything was cleared up. Her thoughts then strayed to Mrs. Rutherford. She hoped the poor woman would have some family to support her. She might have to drop in and give her condolences.

Her body was in autopilot, but her brain was everywhere. She picked up some chrysanthemums, lilies, roses and foliage to create her next order. Halfway through the design she heard a banging on the front display window. It was Jack, her delivery guy.

Sam rushed to the door to let him in.

"What the hell is going on out there?"

"Mr. Rutherford turned up dead in front of the shop."

Jack's eyes went wide like saucers. "How?"

"No idea, and who would do something like that to poor old Mr. Rutherford? The police want me to go in and give a statement."

"I just can't believe it. Bel Haven doesn't have a history of dead bodies suddenly appearing on the street and definitely not a body of an elderly customer."

Jack had a point. This was the first time since she'd been in Bel Haven that something like this had happened.

Jack walked over to the window to look at the commotion outside.

The reporters looked like they'd set up shop for the day. "Get a load of the reporters, they've pulled out the foldable chairs and are drinking coffee."

Samantha rolled her eyes. Now that she didn't need. "How am I supposed to run a business with all that going on?"

Jack shrugged his shoulders. "Could be good publicity."

"Great, I can see it all now. Bewitching Blooms and Murder."

"That might bring some new orders in." He winked.

And right on cue the phone rang.

Jack reached for it. "Bewitching Blooms," he answered with a smile.

Samantha watched in anticipation, hoping it wasn't those pesky reporters.

"Yeah, sure we have stock. I'll pass you on to our head florist."

He held out the phone.

And that was how the rest of morning went. At one point she told Jack to take over the phone orders while she worked to get out as many orders as possible.

"Oh Mr. Rutherford, what have you done?" she whispered. She needed the business but not at his expense. A tear slid down her cheek.

"Want a cup of coffee and some lunch?"

She stabbed a rose into the wet floral foam. Her current arrangement needed a few more flowers to look fuller.

She wanted her customers to feel they were getting good value. "I'd kill for some."

Jack let out a laugh. "Don't let anyone hear you say that."

"Oh, please. Figure of speech and all that."

"Yes, but a bit close to home today. What do you want?"

"The usual."

"Chicken Caesar salad and a small cappuccino with extra chocolate on top?"

"Spot on." She moved from where she'd been working and followed Jack to the front door.

He unlocked it and dashed out.

She turned the lock. It was crazy to keep opening and locking the door, but it was the only way to stop the reporters from asking questions.

She had nothing to say to them because the truth was, she didn't know anything—other than the man that turned up dead as a doornail in front of her shop was a customer. She wanted answers too. She hoped by the time she went to the station this afternoon, someone could at least share something about why he was killed.

A loud thud at the door brought her out of her temporary musing. She turned and took a few steps toward the door, but when she got a look at the guy banging continuously, her feet froze.

He was angry, but he looked lethal in a way that her brain recognized immediately. Her witchy senses tingled. *A warlock.*

Her brain raced. With her defective magic there wasn't anything she could do to stop him if he wanted to zap himself into the shop. The best she'd probably do is blow up the shop and scatter flowers everywhere. The fact that he knocked gave her enough confidence to shake all manner of thoughts from her brain and propel herself forward. With shaky fingers she turned the lock and opened the door. She wedged herself in-between because she wasn't sure whether she wanted him in the shop. "Can I help you?"

"Are you Samantha Willow?"

"I am. Who are you?"

"Lucius Gallo." He bowed.

The pesky reporters had taken the opportunity to follow his lead. She watched over his shoulder. He followed her gaze and turned to the reporters. "There's nothing more to see and report here." He waved his hand.

The reporters retreated with lumbering steps back to their vehicles.

Samantha's brain clicked into gear. His actions and tone told her he wasn't a threat. She pulled the door open and allowed him to enter. She secured the lock again once the warlock was inside.

"Can I get your coat for you?" she asked.

"No, I'm fine."

She studied his face. The five o'clock shadow. He was easily in his late forties with strong features. High cheekbones. She asked, "What can I do for you, Mr. Gallo?"

"Please, just Lucius. I'm here because I think you might be in danger."

Her mouth dropped open. No one in her coven had given a damn about her. Why should this stranger? "My coven has never cared about me. Why should you?"

"Your coven is filled with wannabes who have no clue about half the stuff that goes on in the witch and warlock world."

Her brows rose to her hairline, and her eyes widened. She'd always believed or they had had her believe they were powerful. According to the badass dude in front of her, they were amateurs. She raised her hand. "Wait, wait. Are you saying the coven that tossed me out on my ass isn't as good as they think they are?"

"Now you're catching on." He winked.

"So, what kind of danger do you think I'm in?"

"I'm not sure, but Mr. Rutherford was working for me."

When the context of his words penetrated her brain, her legs became Jell-O. She swayed and reached out to brace herself on the counter, but Lucius grabbed her and held her steady. Her lips were glued tight. No coherent verbiage wanted to come out.

"Let me get you some water."

29

She pointed toward the back of the shop where a small kitchen was housed. She expected Lucius to drop his arms where he held her steady and head in that direction, but he snapped his fingers and a glass of water came sailing through from the rear of the shop and straight to her.

She closed her fingers around it and took a few small slips then cleared her throat. "What do you mean he worked for you?"

"He was tasked when you moved here to keep an eye on you," he said and dropped his hands to his side.

"Were all those flower purchases a sham?"

"No. I don't believe they were."

"And you're saying now someone has done away with him to get to me."

"I believe so."

"But why? I'm defective."

"See, that's where I think you're wrong."

"You have no idea." She concentrated and then got the glass of water to levitate. She flicked her hand so it would move back toward the kitchen. It rose to the ceiling then burst into tiny dust particles.

The warlock raised his hand and her mess disappeared. "Just because you are defective doesn't mean you still can't do damage."

"You know that makes no sense."

"Give it time. You'll work it out."

"Work my magic out?" A rock formed in her belly because she knew it was hopeless. "I've done that. It's ineffective." She waved a hand around the shop. "This is my life."

He stepped closer. "This is a ruse, a guise, not what should be your path."

"It's the only life I know and the only one where I can control what goes on. My magical life is uncontrollable."

"Your life is not the same as it was yesterday and the day before that. Today you have to admit you are a witch, regardless of how much power you have."

He stepped back. "I will return tomorrow." With a twist of his wrist, he was gone.

Chapter Four

S amantha stood staring at the vacant spot that had been occupied by the warlock a few moments ago. To say her morning had been crazy was an understatement. A dead customer, police, annoying reporters and now a warlock with a weird ass story. Her cozy life had just been turned into a soap opera and that was putting it mildly.

Loud banging at the shop front door brought her out of her contemplative state. Her feet shuffled toward the entrance to let Jack back in.

"What happened?" he asked.

"Oh, oh. Nothing. I was off collecting wool."

"I guess it's been a hell of a day."

"You can say that again."

The smell of the chicken Caesar hit her nose and her stomach let out a small growl.

"I think we should tuck into our food." Jack winked.

"No arguments from me. It's probably the most normal thing that's happened around here today." She meant that with every fiber of her being. Dead bodies, police, news reporters and warlocks the day could not get any weirder even if she tried. Samantha moved the flowers from the counter as she usually ate standing but thought she and Jack deserved to sit. "How about we take lunch in the kitchen. The phones and orders can wait for a bit."

They moved to the rear of the shop to the kitchen area. It was small and functional with a four-seater table pushed up against the wall.

She pulled out the chair nearest to her and dropped her weight into it.

Jack put the food in front of her. She stared at it and then dug in.

"Wis is goo," she said with a mouthful of food.

"Yep." Jack nodded his head in agreement. He grabbed one of the bottles of water and washed down some of his food.

"I hope that circus out there beats it."

"You and me both."

The phone at the front of the shop rang. She hadn't brought it with her on purpose. She rolled her eyes. "I better get that."

"Well, let me know what's to be loaded for delivery, and I'll get to it."

"Let me get this then we can work it out." Samantha took another bite of food and got to her feet.

She always said she was a two man show when she spoke about her business. Cliché was putting it mildly. She was happy with it being just her and Jack. They worked well together. They had a silent understanding at times. Of course they spoke about things in their lives, but they didn't pry.

Her fingers closed around the phone, and she hit the answer button. "Hello, this is Bewitching Blooms."

"Hi Samantha, it's Dex, your neighbor."

Images of her early morning interaction with said hot neighbor flashed in her mind. "Oh, hi. What can I do for you?"

"You're all over the news. I wanted to check in and see if you needed help with anything?"

Any help from Dex right now would be a distraction. A pleasant one but still a distraction. Besides, what could he possibly do? It wasn't like he could make that pesky news crew disappear. "No, I'm good. Just a news crew that won't go away. They'll soon enough find out how boring I am and move on."

"There's nothing boring about you, Samantha."

Why did his voice and words make her weak at the knees? She cleared her throat. "Um, thanks for calling Dex. I'm all good."

"Write my number down and if you need anything at all just call me."

She rolled her eyes but entertained him. "Okay. Ready when you are."

He rattled off his number and she scribbled it on the paper.

"Make sure you put that into your cell."

34

"I will."

He hung up.

She let out a sigh. "Get your head back into reality, Sam," she whispered.

"Who was that and why are you all flustered?"

"My seriously hot neighbor." Sam had been privately drooling over him but what the heck, things couldn't get any worse. Might as well share the details about the object of her current fixation.

"Ohh. Spill it," Jack said.

"There's not much to say. He moved in next door over a month ago, and he's, let's just say, pretty much something you see on the cover of one of those fancy magazines." Her face heated. She was oversharing.

"Girl, you've got it bad."

"I've got nothing. He's just my neighbor and nothing more."

"By the look on your face, I'd say you want it to be more."

He wasn't wrong, but guys like Dex never went for clumsy women like Sam. "Okay, I've overshared. Why don't we get back to what we do best, which is, you deliver those orders there." She pointed to a heap of finished bouquets and arrangements. Then flicked her finger across the space. "These are for the event down at More Amore." She walked over to a trolley that was full of table center arrangements.

Jack did a quick scan. "I'll move the van so I can load these up."

"I'll need you to set them up and when you're done, I've got those that need to go too." She nudged her chin to a couple of bouquets made up with note cards.

Jack looked at her. "It's going to be a full day, so I better get moving."

She helped him load the van. When she finished putting the last arrangement in, the sound of boots on the concrete had her turning around fast. A woman who looked familiar with long blonde hair headed her way. *Another reporter*, she thought.

"I don't have anything further to say to you all. You have the most updated information at your fingertips and from the police too."

"I'm not here about that."

"No?" Samantha questioned with slight confusion and embarrassment.

"I wanted to place an order."

"Yeah, sure. Do you want to come into the shop?"

"No, it's okay. I'll just wait out here."

"I'll grab a pen and get your details."

"That would be good."

Samantha dashed inside to get a pen from the counter and some paper. By the time she got back outside the lady was gone.

"Did you see a woman with blonde hair out here?" she asked Jack who had just reappeared.

"Yes."

"Where did she go?"

"Well nowhere, cause she's standing here."

She whacked Jack in the arm. "I'm serious. A woman was just here asking to order flowers. I went in to get a pen and she was gone by the time I came back out."

Jack shrugged his shoulders. "I didn't see anyone, and I best roll."

He had a lot to get through. "Okay."

"Later." He jumped into the van.

She watched Jack drive off and looked up and down the street.

"Wonder who she was and where she went." She whispered to herself.

Chapter Five

From the moment he scented his witchy neighbor, when he moved in, Dex could not erase all manner of thoughts of her from his mind.

This morning only made things worse. It took all his will not to be a cave man and throw her on the floor to give them both the release they needed.

He knew she was just as hot for him as he was for her.

He scented her arousal when she did a slow trace down the contours of his chest and abs.

Damn if that didn't make his dick hard. He wanted her like a starving man.

Dex followed Samantha's shenanigans and all the drama on TV.

He told himself he wouldn't get involved, but his brain had clearly decided not being involved was going against every instinct in his body.

The.

Witch.

Was.

His.

His primal instinct knew it, and it wasn't going to stand by and watch her struggle with all the media and inquiries without support.

He had called his police officer friend to get the inside scoop, and it was clear that whatever was going on, it smelled like a supernatural crime rather than a normal human crime. This also meant his witch had nothing to do with the murder directly, but indirectly someone was trying to send her a message.

His former self had come to the surface, wanting to get involved. He'd left his old job behind for a fresh start from the *Phi Athanatoi*—an immortal group that protected mankind from the evil that lurked at night. He settled here in Bel Haven and worked from home, doing some back-end stuff for Xen Lyson, the head of the *Phi Athanatoi*. This kept the money coming in, but it wasn't about that. He'd built his own fortune over the years, so there was no need for him to work if he didn't want to, but due to his loyalty to Xen he kept his foot in the door.

He'd been doing rather well, and his old life was starting to fizzle into a distant memory. Until he moved here. He knew when he caught a whiff of Samantha there'd be trouble.

He could smell that it followed her. He'd have his hands full and it would make life interesting. The wolf inside growled with appreciation.

He grabbed his keys and headed out. First, he would get rid of the pesky reporters. Then he would see if his witch was okay and sniff out anything that seemed odd. His heightened wolf senses would alert him to anything uncanny.

He drove with purpose, making record time into town. He parked his car far enough away from the reporters. Then got out and headed toward them.

"I heard the suspect for the murder is over in the next town at the All Night Diner," Dex said.

"How do you know this?"

"I have a reliable source."

"Why would you share."

"Hey, I want this guy caught just as much as you do."

The journalist eyed him. "Okay, we're on it. Pack up guys, were heading to the All Night Diner."

They cleared out faster than Dex had thought they would. His wolf inside gave a sly smile.

He crossed the street and headed straight for his witch. He turned his head and scanned the street. *Clear*, he thought then pushed open the door to Bewitching Blooms.

Samantha was at the counter tying off a large bouquet of mixed roses when he stepped inside the shop.

"What a day. That's the last one," she said out loud.

He caught the breath she sucked in when she laid eyes on him and realized she was talking to him. She wasn't immune to him and that pleased his wolf even more. *Calm*, he internalized.

"Dex, what are you doing here?" she asked as he walked toward her.

"I thought I'd drop in and make sure you're okay."

"I... I'm doing fine."

"Looks like your media fans have cleared out." He threw a thumb over his shoulder.

She lifted herself on the balls of her feet to look over Dex's shoulder into the street.

He knew he was wide and tall, but he enjoyed watching her try to see around him.

"You're right, they've taken off. Might have found a new lead?"

"I'd say they have."

"You didn't have to come in."

"I just wanted to make sure things had settled down. The cameras have been pointing at your shop all morning."

Her face heated, and he caught how that changed her scent. "I'm the joke of Bel Haven."

Dex stepped forward. "You are no joke, Samantha."

He wanted nothing more than to pull her to him and crash his lips to hers. *Calm down.* He scolded his inner beast for wanting to act like a barbarian. It seemed this witch was wreaking havoc on his mind and body.

41

He was sure any other wolf would think the witch cast a spell on him, but he recognized her for what she was—his mate.

She cleared her throat and brought him out of his own inner musings.

"I'm grateful you came by, Dex. You really didn't need to."

Oh, he needed to. His witch didn't know she needed his help, yet. The wolf inside roared. *Ours.* He couldn't agree more.

"There's no telling when those reporters might come back."

He knew they wouldn't because by the time they discovered his tip was nothing more than a wild goose chase, Samantha would be back home where he could keep an eye and ear out for her from next door.

She scrunched up her nose, and that made her look all the more adorable. *Down boy.*

"Well, I'm about to clean up and then head to the police station."

"I'm coming with you. You might need some support."

"Honestly, Dex, I'm okay."

"I would prefer to see you to your door and make sure you aren't being harassed."

"Trust me, they didn't harass me much. Officer Andor managed to shoo them away." She waved her hands.

It gave him comfort that Andor had helped. He knew him well.

Another wolf who worked with the *Phi Athanatoi.*

They had people all over the globe in various authoritative roles to help with the weird cases humans couldn't figure out or explain.

"I am grateful you popped in to help, but I should be okay."

He wouldn't push the issue. "Where's your phone?"

"Why?"

He raised an eyebrow at her. Her reaction told him she hadn't stored his number. "Get me your phone."

She shuffled stuff around the counter and closed her fingers around her cell phone that had been under some cellophane. "I didn't get a chance..."

He stepped toward her and snatched it out of her hands. His fingers flew over the phone. "I know," he said, handing the phone back. His fingers brushed hers, and it sent an electric shock through him. His inner wolf rose to the surface. *Mine.* "Send me a message when you get home."

"There really isn't any need."

He leaned in to inhale and whisper in her ear. "Oh, there's plenty of need."

He turned on his heels and headed out the door before he did something he would regret. Easy boy. *You need to woo her first.* His logic knew what was right, but his primal side wanted nothing more than to claim the witch. His witch, and he would fight anyone who caused her grief.

He dashed across the road and scanned the streets.

The reporters wouldn't be back anytime soon and when they did return, there'd be no one to watch.

Hopefully by tomorrow their attention would be focused elsewhere.

He got into his car and headed for home. There was work to do. He had to find out who murdered Samantha's customer. Something didn't sit right with him. Either someone was trying to send a message to the witch or something far more sinister was going on.

He drove with purpose, weaving through traffic like a mini obstacle course. He knew it wasn't a full moon, but man the drivers on the road this evening were on the crazy side. Even driving with the window down he could smell the shift in the air. He needed to make some calls, and the first call would be to his old boss, Xen Lyson, the head of the *Phi Athanatoi*. Xen was a vampire and had lived for many millennia. Naturally wolves didn't live as long as vampires, but they did get a good run. Xen's organization had supernatural beings spread across the globe. When Dex had moved into his house a delicate scent hit his nose from the backyard, and everything in him had screamed to jump over and possess the female it belonged to. It took all his willpower to calm his inner emotions. A primitive beast he was not, but boy did he want to be.

He pulled into his driveway, put the car in park and made his way into the house and to his office. He wasted no time firing up his laptop and sending off a few emails.

He fished out his phone and called the one person he didn't think he'd be calling so soon.

"Bored already?" Xen asked him.

He grunted. "Not by a long shot."

"What do you need?"

"I think there's something going on here."

"You only just got there. Do you need some men?"

"No. I've got Caspian and Eric if needed." Both men were capable in Dex's estimation. If there were a need to escalate, he wouldn't hesitate. "I wanted to ask if you could get me a list of witches and warlocks in Bel Haven."

"I'll get Adam to send through what we have in the database."

"Thanks, Xen. I appreciate it."

"You might want to tell me what this is about."

Dex paused, thinking about whether to share with the vampire or wait until he had worked out who he was dealing with. "I found my mate, and I think she may be a target of some witches."

"You know we have the ability to stamp out anything minor going on with the covens there. I don't need to tell you we have a powerful witch on our side, and if you think you need me personally..."

"No, no, Xen. It's nothing of that magnitude."

"You know we're only a phone call away, *lykos*." He used the Greek term for wolf.

"I know, Xen. Thank you." He hung up. He wouldn't bring the heavy artillery in unless he needed to. Right now, all he needed was Xen's information on what witches and warlocks were in Bel Haven. There wasn't a supernatural creature Xen didn't have a one pager on.

Dex's laptop pinged. He had the information he wanted. He scanned it quickly and stopped scrolling on Samantha's page. Orphaned at a young age and taken in by her coven. Her powers were not a threat. In fact, his mate was a klutz. He smiled. He could envisage life with Samantha. She'd certainly kept him on his toes, and for some strange reason, he didn't mind the mayhem that could potentially follow her around. *Would keep things interesting.* He mused.

He typed a group message. He needed the boys over for beers and a much needed catch up on what had been going on in town as well as intel on the current murder at Sam's front door.

"Sam." He tested it out loud. He liked how it sounded.

Chapter Six

The police station was buzzing when Sam pulled up in her van. She parked her vehicle. "I hope it doesn't take too long," she whispered under her breath as she pulled the keys out of the ignition and rummaged around the back to grab her bag. She was bone-tired. A knock at her window startled her. It was the same warlock from earlier in the day, and his face meant business.

With shaky hands she stuck her keys in the ignition and then pressed the button for the window to lower. "Why are you here?"

"I wanted to warn you not to say anything about our conversation."

She held her finger up to indicate he should wait a moment. She pulled the door open and stepped outside. "I'm not that stupid, and if I said a warlock popped in to see me, then that would make me sound stupid."

He held his hands up in surrender. "That's not what I meant."

"Listen buster, I don't care what you or the magical community thinks. You all turned your backs on me a long time ago. It's unfortunate that a nice man like Mr. Rutherford is dead. I knew him as a customer, and that's all I can tell the police or anyone else for that matter because that's the truth. The whole truth and nothing but the truth."

"You're not on the stand."

"I may not be but you..." she pointed a finger at his chest, "... sneaking around to tell me what to say may very well put me there."

"Samantha, I didn't mean to upset you, only to warn you to use caution till we find out who killed him, and you know it's not an ordinary human death."

"Well, how was I supposed to know? I've never seen a dead man on my front doorstep before."

The warlock stepped forward and put his hands on her arms. She lifted her head up.

"I didn't mean to upset you. I know you had a hard day, and my sudden appearance didn't help matters. I deeply regret coming here tonight."

She saw the sincerity written on his face. She had lost her shit. It had been a bad day and now the only thought running through her head was that she had made a complete boob of herself.

"I'm sorry, I didn't mean to snap. It's been a crazy kind of day."

Lucius let go of her arms. "It has."

"Look, there's nothing I could possibly say. I wasn't near the shop when it happened. So there's nothing more to elaborate on. I have already told them what I know, and that's pretty close to nothing."

Lucius watched her for a minute. "I'm sorry to have riled you up. I should let you get on with your business without intervention. However, if you do find yourself in trouble, just say my name."

She nodded before moving toward the station. The hairs on the nape of her neck had risen. She spun around only to find the warlock gone. "Can this day get any crazier?" she huffed under her breath. Sam entered the busy foyer of the station and walked up to the counter.

"Can I help you, ma'am?"

"Yes, I'm looking for Detective Nicholls and Officer Andor."

"Give me a minute." The desk officer punched a few numbers on her phone. Her hair was pulled back in a tight bun.

"What's your name, ma'am?"

"Samantha Willow."

"Are Nicholls and Andor with you?"

Silence.

"Uha, uha. Okay." She dropped the phone back in place.

"They left an hour ago. What did you want to see them about?"

"They told me to come by and give a statement."

The desk officer looked at her.

"Um... in regard to the murder in front of my shop."

"Okay, well, I can help you there. Just come with me."

She led Sam to a small room. "Take a seat. This will be video recorded. One of the officers will ask you a bunch of questions." She turned and left the room, leaving the door open.

Sam let out a long breath of frustration. She leaned back and stared at the ceiling. She had fought hard for some sort of ordinary life. Why was all this happening now? Maybe Lucius was right. Maybe she was in danger. Maybe somebody had it in for her. The only problem was she didn't mix in the circles of her own kind. Lucius was the first warlock she'd seen in ages.

"Ahem."

She snapped out of her musing and turned to the door.

Folder in hand, a large officer sat down opposite her. "I'm Officer Jacob Tubbs, and you are..." he flipped the file open, "... Samantha Willow."

She nodded her head. "Yes, that's correct."

"Okay. I'm going to record this."

"No problem."

Officer Tubbs hit the record button on a little remote control that sat on the table.

"Where were you last night?"

"At home with my dog."

"Can anyone vouch for you?"

Sam was about to shake her head and say no, but she remembered the whole kitchen window scene with Dex."

"My neighbor Dex can. He saw me through the kitchen window." She thought about it for a second. "That sounds creepy, doesn't it?"

"Not at all. I've heard stranger things at this station. Go on."

"I was washing up in my kitchen and I saw my neighbor. He saw me too."

"Does Dex have a surname."

"I'm not sure. He only recently moved in."

"I've got your shop address here. What's your home address?"

And that was how the next hour went. She tried really hard not to yawn and apologized when two slipped out. When they wrapped it up, he walked her out to the foyer that was now empty and looked at her. "Why do I get the feeling you've somehow been thrown in the path of danger?"

She ran through a few responses in her head. "I only knew the man as a customer, why someone would deliberately drop him on my doorstep is beyond me." There, that sounded good. Although she knew from Lucius that someone was trying to send a message. Mr. Rutherford was after all working for Lucius and keeping an eye on her. Someone had found out. That much was evident, but this was not a human matter.

This was a supernatural matter, and when the lines of both worlds collided, things got complicated. She'd had to go along with what the human police wanted.

"Thank you again for coming down."

"Just doing my duty. Besides, this sort of thing doesn't happen in Bel Haven."

"No, it's not something that happens often, but we do get a lot of crazy, and crazier stuff has been amping up these last couple of months. Makes me think there must be something in the water."

She let out a laugh. "Maybe there is."

"Take care."

"Thank you, good night." She waved at Officer Tubbs and headed to her car. The first thing she did when she got inside was lock the doors. For some reason the day had left her feeling paranoid. "Hope I don't turn into one of those people who looks over their shoulders every five minutes."

"I'm sure you won't."

She jumped in her seat. Her heart pounded so hard against her chest.

Lucius was in the passenger seat.

"What on earth?"

"I just need to know that you will get home safe."

"If you stop popping in and out, I might." She put her hand on her heart.

"I need you to understand that witches and warlocks don't always play fair. They would not give you a second glance before eliminating you."

"I get it. Witches and warlocks with power can kill me. If that's what they want, why haven't they done it yet?"

"That's my question too. Maybe it's something else they seek. Something they need through you?"

"Well, there's nothing, remember? I'm an orphan." She put the key in the ignition and started the van. The sooner she got home the sooner she'd lose Lucius. She'd had enough of this nonsense for one day.

"Good point," Lucius said.

She really wanted to say *duh* but thought that would be too childish. She sped down the empty streets of Bel Haven with a single purpose. To get home, have food, a shower and to ultimately get some rest.

"I want to ward your house when you get home."

"Won't that be pointless to other witches and warlocks?"

"Yes, if your spell is weak anyone will be able to penetrate it."

"I'm guessing there's a 'but' in there."

"Indeed."

Samantha wasn't going to argue with him. One thing she knew without having seen his full power in action was that you didn't want to mess with him. The man had presence and then some.

She pulled up into her driveway, put the car in park and switched off the engine. She had barely enough time to look over to Lucius before he hopped out.

She rolled her eyes. "I hope this isn't a new norm." Reaching over to the back seat she pulled her handbag to her lap. Lucius was at her front door, waving his arms about like some lunatic, but Samantha knew that whatever spell he was concocting, nothing would get in without hitting difficulty.

She stood near him and followed the energy whisps of magic; she could see it. Holographic runes etched into the door. Her mouth dropped open. "Who would have thought?"

He finished his spell and turned toward her. "It saddens me that you never had the right training."

A spear shot straight to her chest. She too wished her coven had treated her in a similar fashion as the other kids. She shook her head. She didn't want to relieve those nasty years. They were behind her.

"Do you have any friends who visit you on a regular basis?"

"Yes."

"What are their names?"

"There's Ellie and Jack."

"Two people?" He raised an eyebrow at her.

"Well, I'm still new."

He huffed.

"Oh, and there's Dex next door."

He spoke the names and the runes on the door glowed thrice before disappearing altogether. "Your house is now warded from any witch, warlock or other creature. Only you can invite whom you want in. Humans are the exception—they can enter without an invitation."

Her brain took a moment to catch up. She was certain she hadn't heard him right but asked anyway. "What other creatures?"

"You'd be surprised what's out there," he said winking before dematerializing from her porch.

She stood there with her mouth open for a moment. A shiver ran down her spine, and she shook it off. The warlock was clearly mad. She rummaged through her bag for her keys. As soon as she inserted the key, Gilbert started to bark from behind the door. He jumped up and down her legs the minute she crossed the threshold. "Okay, boy. I missed you too." She dropped to her knees, letting her bag slide down her shoulder. She petted him and he licked her face. "Whoa, you really did miss me today." She cuddled him a bit and placed a few kisses on his head. "Come on, let's go get some dinner." Gilbert yapped loudly with approval.

She collected her bag and dropped it on a side table near the staircase.

Then she shucked her shoes off and headed straight to the kitchen.

She'd pick them up later. She was too tired to care.

She pulled the freezer open and pulled out some frozen bolognaise she'd cooked and frozen for quick meals. "I think it's a pasta night." She got a pot, dropped the bolognaise in and added water so it wouldn't burn on the bottom. Then she filled another pot with water. Gilbert was still weaving himself between her legs. "What's gotten into you?"

He let out another bark. "Come on, let's get you something. She grabbed some dog food and put it in Gilbert's bowl.

He barked and turned his nose up.

No matter how many times she tried to get him to eat that stuff, he always reacted the same way. She swore sometimes Gilbert was anything but a regular dog. He had a mind of his own, or so it seemed. "Okay, you want to wait for the pasta, or do you want leftovers?"

He trotted to the fridge.

"Leftovers it is." She pulled out a plate with two pieces of steak. She cut them into small pieces before putting them down on the floor for Gilbert. He didn't waste time. "A bit hungry, eh?" She asked while he chewed.

She walked over to tend to her dinner and just as she was putting the pasta in the boiling water she heard loud music coming from Dex's house. She peered out the window. Sure enough, he was having a party. Could this day get worse? Now she'd have a sleep deprived night due to loud music. She felt a pang of disappointment. It would have been nice to have had an occasion to go to.

Lucius' comments at the front door about her number of friends had hit a nerve. She knew she didn't have a large circle of people around her, but some of that was intentional. She didn't trust her coven and the less people she mixed with the less chance someone could report where she'd taken off too. She liked the quiet life she had built in Bel Haven. Lost in her thoughts, she realized dinner was ready to plate up and eat.

Gilbert had finished eating. Full and content he dropped at her feet while she ate with the sound of Dex's music pumping from next door. She remembered her promise to check in. She sent him a text and waited for a reply. There was nothing. "Obviously too busy having a good time," she said looking down at Gilbert.

She didn't linger waiting for him to text back. She rinsed the plates, stacked them in the dishwasher and sorted the leftovers.

Gilbert was already taking the stairs as she rounded the corner to head up for bed. She contemplated a shower, but she was dead on her feet. She changed into a comfy t-shirt and dropped into her bed. Her phone pinged. An emoji from her hot neighbor. A thumbs up.

Sleep wrapped itself around her to the tune of Dex's music.

Chapter Seven

Samantha startled awake from a dream. Gilbert sat upright and barked. She rolled over and cracked her eyelid open. It was seven. She needed to hustle if she was going to get to work. Saturdays were slow days and opening time was ten. "Urgh. I could just sleep in."

Gilbert barked in agreement.

She got to her feet and headed for the shower. She could hear commotion from Dex's house. His party crowd must have been too drunk to leave. Another pang hit her in the gut. She let out a frustrated breath. "What's wrong with you, Sam? Just because he's your neighbor doesn't mean he has to invite you."

She finished showering and dressing with her thoughts on Dex. She was sure she was misinterpreting his reaction toward her because she liked him.

She made coffee and headed to the backyard to catch a few morning rays of sunshine.

She sat at her outdoor setting, and the noise next door amped up another notch to loud cheering. She rolled her eyes. It sounded like they were playing some sort of game.

Football.

Another loud cheer sounded moments later. She took a sip of coffee and wondered if Dex had family in Bel Haven and maybe that was why he'd moved here. The plates on his car were from Virginia. She hadn't missed any details about her sometimes-shirtless neighbor. She was certain Mrs. Dravis, across the road, would be blushing red seeing Dex shirtless while taking out the trash.

She took another sip of coffee, thinking about said neighbor. Gilbert started barking and racing around the backyard and sticking his nose close to Dex's fence. She got to her feet to get him back into the house. An airborne torpedo came hurtling toward her.

Witch's brew. She didn't give it much thought. She raised her hand and focused on a spell to repel the ball.

"*Recedo*," she whispered.

The ball didn't do as she'd desired. Instead it sped up and before she could try something else it hit her straight in the face, and she dropped like a sack of potatoes to the ground with a loud pained noise reaching her ears.

Her scream of pain.

Her world spun, and the last thing she heard was Gilbert barking like crazy and commotion from Dex's fence line.

Someone was patting her face.

She opened her eyes to see Dex mouthing something. Her eyes and ears were not in sync.

"Samantha, are you okay?"

Gilbert licked her face.

"Let me call an ambulance."

She turned her head to the other voice. She raised her finger to point to Officer Andor.

"I'm already on it," Detective Nicholls confirmed.

"What are they doing here?"

"They're with me."

"Oh." She dropped her arm, which had suddenly gained a ton of weight.

"Let's get you inside."

Before she could protest, Dex lifted her into his arms and tucked her to him. His strong hard chest felt good. She wanted nothing more than to just curl into him.

Dex let out a moan. He walked them back into the house and through to her living room. Gilbert was yapping all the way.

"I'm fine, I'll be fine." She was trying to be brave. She lifted her hand to her nose to wipe it, something wet coated her fingers–blood.

"I'd rather be sure," Dex said.

The cops hadn't followed Dex in. That was odd. "Where are your friends?"

"At the door."

She remembered what Lucius had said about other creatures not being able to enter because of his ward. Surely he'd put too much spell on the house since even the cops couldn't come in. Maybe something went wrong with his spell. She didn't give it much thought. She shouted, "Detective Nicholls and Officer Andor, please come in."

She heard the heavy footsteps of the two men approach where she lay.

"How's she doing?" Officer Andor asked.

"Seems a little out of it, but okay," Dex said.

"I noticed the security is A level," Nicholls said.

"What security?" she asked.

They all looked down at her until a knock at the door had them scattering to answer it.

Her head hurt.

Gilbert nuzzled on the couch with her, and she patted him. He let out a concerned whine.

"She's through here," she heard Dex say.

"Is this your wife?" the paramedic asked.

Samantha was lucid enough to answer. "No. He's just my hot neighbor." A second later she realized that *hot* did not belong in that sentence. She scrambled to correct herself. "I mean neighbor."

The paramedic leaned over and whispered. "I know what you mean." She winked. "Now let's have a look at you." She rummaged in her bag for gloves.

"What happened?"

"She got hit by our football," Dex answered.

"It's totally my fault," Andor said. "I was the one who kicked it."

The paramedic looked up Sam's nose. "The bleeding has stopped, which is good." Then with gloved hands she pressed around the affected area ever so gently. "Good news for you ma'am, it doesn't appear to be broken. I recommend you see your doctor. If you're in pain over the next few days or your nose swells, or if you have trouble breathing from your nasal passages, it means you need an X-ray. Keep an eye on it. Take some Tylenol for the pain."

Sam tried to sit up. Her head spun, and Dex was there in seconds to assist her. "I'll get you some water. Where do you keep the Tylenol?"

"In the cupboard above the sink."

The paramedic cleaned her up. And rechecked everything. The area was tender, and Sam let out a tiny hiss.

"Put some ice on it. Then get it assessed by your doctor."

Dex came back with a glass of water, Tylenol and an icepack.

"Great minds." The paramedic pointed to the icepack in Dex's hand.

"Figured she might need it."

The paramedic winked at Dex and turned. "Fellas."

Sam watched as she nodded at the boys before leaving.

Dex gave her the water and medication and then the ice pack.

"Thank you, Dex." Her brain did a backpedal.

Boys—when did she induct them into some sort of group? They were the police and Dex's friends. Not hers. Andor followed the paramedic out and then returned.

"Okay, thank you. I'll be fine from here."

Gilbert chose that moment to bark.

"I'm staying to make sure you're all right," Dex said.

"You don't understand. I need to get to work."

"Not like this you're not."

"I think it's time Andor and I took off."

"I'm really sorry about that ball hitting you." Ander's shoulders dropped.

She held up her hand. If she hadn't tampered with it, it might have missed her altogether, but no, she had to try to use her pathetic and defective magic.

"Look, it's okay, Officer Andor."

"Please call me Eric."

"Eric, don't feel bad about it. Things like this happen all the time. If I hadn't gotten up to chase Gilbert, the ball would have missed me by a mile." She paused. "Okay, maybe not a mile, but you know what I mean."

"Still, I feel bad. What can we do to help? You said you had to go to work. Do you need a hand?"

Dex let out a small growl in Eric's direction.

He stuck his hands up in surrender. "I'm here to help. That's all."

Samantha considered everything for a second. It was more drama than she needed. Time to defuse things and get rid of everyone. "Thank you, Eric, but I'm good."

"Dex, thank you for bringing me inside and Detec..."

"It's Caspian."

"Right. Thank you for calling the paramedics. Now, if you'll all excuse me, I'd like to freshen up and get moving."

"Again, sorry Samantha." Eric and Caspian took their leave.

Sam eyed Dex. "You too. Scoot."

"You just got torpedoed by a football. I'm not scooting anywhere."

She got to her feet and the room spun.

Strong arms pulled her close. "I've got you," Dex said, holding her tight. "Now you see why you can't go in."

"I have to Dex. There're orders I need to fill."

"How about you rest for a couple of hours and see how you go? I'll drive you in myself."

She thought about it. It sounded like a plan, and she nodded her head in agreement.

"Atta girl."

Gilbert started barking.

Dex sat her back down on the couch, and Gilbert jumped over her legs and licked her face.

Dex let out a laugh. "Looks like he wants some attention."

She gave him a cuddle as he settled beside her.

"I'm going to go clean up the mess at my place and then I'll be back to check on you."

She wanted some space and the only way to get it was to agree. "Okay."

He leaned in. His face close to hers. "Don't do anything." He patted Gilbert, and her dog lapped it up, even licking Dex's hands. Without another word Dex made his way to the front door and let himself out, leaving her with her thoughts and Gilbert.

She lay down and hoped she could just be normal. If she had normal witch power the football would not have hit her, and there wouldn't have been any drama. She slowly unpacked the events in her mind. One thing bothered her—Eric and Caspian couldn't enter her house until she'd invited them in. She remembered what Lucius had said about the spell. "Creatures," she voiced. They couldn't enter because they weren't entirely human. "What the?" She sat upright, and a number of thoughts cascaded through her mind. What had she done? She didn't know these guys well, and she'd just given them permission to come and go. "Oh damn." The paramedic was definitely human as she hadn't needed an invitation.

They were Dex's friends, and he hadn't shown any sign of aggression. In fact, the opposite, and come to think of it, Eric and Caspian could have used any opportunity yesterday to attack her if they were after her. If anything, they had the perfect opportunity when the ball hit her. No, no.

They were something else. Deep down she knew they were not after her. What were they? She puzzled.

All her childhood memories came rushing back. The mistreatment from her coven to some of the classes taught about not just the witch's world but the supernatural world. Some good, some bad. Demons were bad. Vampires and werewolves were a witch's mortal enemy, or so they were taught repeatedly. Up until now, she hadn't believed they existed because she'd had yet to cross paths with either.

"Maybe they were stories told just to keep us in line," she said to Gilbert .

He let out a whimper that sounded a lot like, *you just keep telling yourself that.*

A spike of adrenaline ignited through her body when she heard a knock on the front door.

"Some guard dog you are." She patted Gilbert and got up to answer the door. It was Dex. She took a sharp intake of breath. *Witch's brew…* she thought he was hot without his shirt, but he looked even better in his black denim pants and untucked shirt.

Dex grinned. "Are you going to let me in or stand there and ogle at me?"

Her mouth dropped open to give some excuse but figured she'd sound ridiculous trying to prove she wasn't staring when in fact she was. She stepped aside and did a low sweep with her arm so he could enter. "I believe you know the way."

He smiled. Maybe entertained by her antics.

She closed the door and followed behind. "Just for your information, I wasn't ogling."

He stopped, but she didn't get that memo and crashed into a hard wall. History was going to repeat itself. Dex spun on the balls of his feet and swept her into an embrace.

She looked up at him.

"Don't fight it, Samantha. We both want the same thing."

Her phone chose that moment to shrill like a banshee. "I have to get that. It'll be Jack wondering where I am."

"I'm coming with you, and I won't take no for an answer."

She didn't know why but her body agreed. Heat pooled low in her belly.

"Careful. It won't take me much to lose control."

She cleared her throat and pushed herself out of Dex's embrace. It only took a fleeting second for her to miss the warmth from his body. What was it about that man?

She padded to the kitchen to pick up the shrilling banshee.

Jack's name was on the screen. She swiped to answer. "You'd better get down here."

Chapter Eight

They pulled to the front of Bewitching Blooms and a massive line-up snaked all the way down the street.

"What on earth?" The saying had become her go-to phrase these last couple of days. She said it again as she turned off the van's engine. "What on earth?"

"Even bad publicity is good publicity," Dex said.

"I don't have the staff or stock to serve all those people."

"I'll control the crowd. You deal with what you can inside."

She looked over at Dex. Who was this man?

They got out of the vehicle. People in front of her door were taking photos.

Dex walked directly to the crowd and told them to delete the photos. It helped that he was tall and wide.

Jack was waiting outside. "It's madness."

"You're telling me." She unlocked the door and pushed it open.

Loud cheers erupted.

"What the hell is that about?" Samantha asked.

"I guess they want flowers." Jack put his hand out so Samantha could hand over her bag.

"Thanks."

He took them through to the back kitchen area and returned to the front. There were a few deliveries she'd made up yesterday in the fridge, ready to go. "Want to load the orders, and then I can deal with this? Could use you to do some of the smaller stuff too."

"No problem, Sam." He pointed out front. "I take it your security detail is your neighbor."

A heated flush reached her cheeks.

"Well, look at you. All shy. You got it bad girl."

"Jack... stop teasing."

He walked to the fridge for the orders, put them on a trolley to load the van.

Samantha pulled her floral apron over her head as the bell on the door rang.

It was Dex. "Are you ready?"

"As ready as I'll ever be."

"I'm going to send them in one at a time unless you tell me otherwise."

"Okay. Send in the first customer."

The first ten customers just wanted small bouquets of flowers and a chance to see where Mr. Rutherford had died.

A pang hit her every time someone brought up his name. Everyone asked what the police were doing about it, and every time she answered in the same way.

"I'm sure they're working on it as we speak."

"Are there any leads?" Mrs. Bates, from the Cake Shop across the road, asked. "I worried for you when I saw all the police yesterday."

"No need to worry, Mrs. Bates. I'm okay, and it's a terrible shock to the community."

"Yes, yes. I haven't seen anything like this in over thirty years."

She went on about how Bel Haven was a good place to raise a family and how things had changed.

Sam zoned in and out of the conversation. Sadly, she did that with a few of her customers. She didn't want to be rude—they were buying flowers, and she was making money from them, but truth be told they just wanted gossip.

At about 3:30 she'd had enough. She walked to the front door where Dex stood facing out. He covered most of it with his width and height. "Can I have a word with you?"

"Sure." He entered the shop. "What's up?"

"I don't know about you, but I need some lunch, and Jack isn't due back for another hour."

"Tell me what you feel like?"

"Maybe just a sandwich to get me through."

His phone appeared lightning fast. He looked at her from under his lashes while poised to make a call. "You didn't have breakfast because of the ball incident. You've been working since we got here, non-stop. A sandwich isn't going to cut it."

He was right, but she didn't want to admit it. She scrunched up her nose and twitched it. A bucket of flowers levitated and then dropped. "Uh-oh."

"Not to be cliché, but I guess the cat's out of the bag, witch."

She wanted to run. Ice ran through her veins. Her defective magic had just exposed her to Dex.

He stepped closer and pulled her to him. "Do not fear me. I've known since I met you."

Her mouth dried. "But... but."

"I'm wolf, Samantha, and you're mine."

She took a big gulp. What the heck was happening in her life? Dead people, warlocks showing up, wolves. Her mouth dropped open. "That can't be true."

"Why?"

"Wolves aren't real?"

"And witches are?"

He had her there. "It does kind of sound stupid to say you don't exist and I do."

"Yes, it does."

"So, you're not scared I might turn you into a toad?"

He let out a deep rumbly laugh that traveled all the way down to her belly. It was the first time she'd heard him laugh and she liked it, a lot.

"I'm not afraid of you, Samantha. You're mine."

"Possessive, much?" She raised an eyebrow in question. "That's the second time you've said that. I'm trying to work out if you're a complete Neanderthal or just plain Alpha male."

"Definitely both when I'm around you."

She digested the whole exchange. "Where do we go from here?"

His lips crashed to hers. Then sought entrance. She granted him that because she wanted the same thing. Heat pooled low in her belly. Dex didn't kiss her, he consumed her, each stroke of his tongue desperate like she was. She was his lifeline and he hers.

Outside the crowd erupted in cheers.

She broke the kiss and Dex let out a growl.

"Stay here. I'll get rid of them and then we can have some lunch, but I'd rather have you."

Her heart ran a marathon. She must have been in some alternate universe because guys like Dex didn't belong with defective witches. How he believed she belonged to him was beyond her. She'd have to set him straight. He had his wires crossed.

She put together another bouquet while Dex busied himself outside with the mob.

A few had tried to get in, but when Dex stepped in front of the shop door, they backed away. She let out a giggle, lucky he was there. Otherwise she wouldn't be able to move in the shop.

True to his word the customers were clearing out. She was thankful for the business, but in her normal world they wouldn't all be purchasing flowers if it wasn't for the murder of Mr. Rutherford.

Dex entered the store again. "The food should be here in ten minutes."

She was sure her stomach now growled.

"Want me to clear your counter?"

"There's a small kitchen through there."

"Good. Let me help you clean up."

The bell on the door rang. "Where did everyone go?" Jack said.

"Dex cleared them out so we could eat in peace."

Dex gave her a look that said he wanted to eat her.

She shook her head, thinking she'd misunderstood his reaction.

The shop door opened again, and this time it was their food. Dex pulled out some cash and handed it to the delivery guy. "We should sit down and eat before it gets cold."

Before they could get to it, Lucius popped in and madness erupted.

Jack screamed.

Dex growled and shifted into a wolf in front of their eyes, which made Jack scream again and fall into the flower display. He toppled over and took a few bunches with him.

Lucius ducked when Dex jumped in his direction, but Dex managed to bite into Lucius' arm. Droplets of blood stained Lucius' clothing. Dex growled and was ready to attack Lucius again.

Samantha stepped in front of Lucius and stuck her hands out. "Dex, stop it."

He growled but stayed put.

"He's not an enemy."

Jack managed to get himself to his feet. "That's a wolf. He, he, he..." He raised a finger to Dex and shook his head. "I should really lay off those chili dogs."

"It's real, Jack. I'll explain in a minute." Samantha looked over to Dex.

He was watching her but also Lucius. He didn't look convinced.

"Trust me."

Dex let out a long whine and disappeared down the corridor to the kitchen. A moment later footsteps sounded, and he appeared. He had a towel hanging from his hips.

Samantha's mouth dropped open. The man should be illegal. She tingled in places she shouldn't.

It was clear Dex hadn't missed her reaction. Small lines appeared around his lips. He liked it.

"Okay. We all need to talk."

"I don't know about y'all, but I think I need to go home and lie down," Jack said.

"Not until I explain. I'd do a little hocus pocus on you, but it might backfire as I'm defective."

Dex stepped closer to her. "There's nothing defective about you, Samantha."

"The wolf is right," Lucius agreed.

"Wait. Wolf, hocus pocus? What are you saying, Sam, that you're a witch?" Jack's eyes widened.

She nodded. "Yep, it's true and you're not crazy."

"I want to run screaming. Is weird that I feel compelled to stay and hear it out."

"Now that we've cleared that up." Dex stepped into Lucius' space. "Who are you and what are you doing here?"

"My name is Lucius, and I have been keeping an eye on Samantha since she lost her parents."

Dex's shoulders relaxed an inch. "Why does she need protection?"

Actually, that was a good question and something Sam was beginning to wonder herself.

"Samantha's magical bloodline goes back farther than most of the witches in the coven she was placed in. You could say witches often fear magic blood older than theirs."

"But I'm defective. I couldn't cast a spell if my life depended on it." And witches and warlocks, had she ever tried.

But she couldn't get one thing to work, so she had all but given up. That was why she'd relocated to Bel Haven. This was her life now. "I have a life here. I don't want anything to do with any coven."

"That may be so, but it doesn't change what they're thinking or what they want to think. The danger is real," Lucius emphasized.

"Then why don't you just use your power on them? You said they were amateurs in comparison to other witches and warlocks."

"Because you can't change village mentality," Dex added. "They're at the pitchfork level, and they won't back down..."

"Till she's dead or gone," Lucius interrupted.

"Do you know who and how many?" Dex asked.

"There's at least one coven involved. Fortunately for now, it appears it's not Samantha's old one. I suspect whoever has his or her sights on Sam is from higher up in the chain. The spell used to kill Mr. Rutherford, who worked for me, was dark magic."

"Dark magic?" Sam asked.

"There are those who seek to obtain more potent powers. The trouble with dark magic is it corrupts and consumes the user. It's why witches and wizards stamped out its use hundreds of years ago." Lucius stepped closer to Sam. "Whoever is coming after you, isn't going to rest."

"The witch is mine and I will protect her."

Lucius raised an eyebrow. "Well, I didn't see that coming."

"What do you mean by that?" Sam asked.

"Yeah, what Sam asked?" Jack quizzed. No doubt confused about everything he'd seen and heard.

"There was a need to place special wards around your shop. To stop any other magical people entering. There's no knowing for sure if those who enter are friends or foe. It's for the best. I popped in to tell you when your mate decided to pounce."

"Mate?"

"I'll let him explain."

"This is better than TV." Jack seemed amused by it all. "Better than Teen Wolf."

Sam gave Jack a look. His smile turned serious.

A loud explosion sounded from outside the shop.

Sam glanced out the window to see a ball of fire. "My van!" She ran to the door.

Chapter Nine

Two strong arms pulled Sam back and into a rock-hard chest. "I strongly suggest you stay in here. You don't know if someone's out there waiting for you."

"I agree," Lucius said.

"I agree, agree," Jack piped in.

"Warlock, can you give me some suitable attire?" Dex released her.

Lucius gave a flick of his wrist and Dex was fully clothed.

Dex turned to Samantha and Jack. "Both of you stay here. I'm going to call Nicholls and Andor. Remember to invite them in. They're on our side."

"What are they?" Sam asked.

"Same as me."

She digested the fact that there was more than one wolf in Bel Haven. "Any others?" she asked.

"No." Dex picked up his phone from the floor. "I'll be outside."

"I'll join you. I need to look around." Lucius walked to the door.

Sam and Jack watched as the fire trucks screeched to a halt outside her shop.

"So much drama in two days," she huffed.

"Life just got a hell of a lot more interesting."

"Jack, I liked my quiet life."

"Yes, but your quiet wasn't as hot as that Alpha wolf out there."

"Shut up, Jack."

"Hmmm. You know I'm right."

"Can I ask you something?"

"Yeah, sure."

"Why is it you accepted this..." she waved her hand around "... whole witches and wolves thing so easily. I mean, I know you freaked out when Dex shifted, but why didn't you run?"

"Funny you ask. I almost did but then something in my brain sparked a memory."

"From your childhood?"

"Yeah. My mom used to say sometimes that she worked for a witch and warlock, but I always thought she was joking.

Then one morning while we were having breakfast, this witch and warlock popped into our house.

So, they were real after all. Did a few tricks but I was just a kid and I always put it down to an overactive imagination because it was the first and last time I saw them."

"You never saw them again? Did your mom stop working for them?"

"No, they just disappeared apparently." He shrugged his shoulders. "My mom always thought something terrible happened to them."

"I wonder what happened?"

"They may have moved to another town. I remember something about trouble with other witches and warlocks. Who's to say, maybe they had a falling out."

"Looks like that's a constant in the magical world."

"Not wrong there."

They watched the drama unfold on the street. The news crew was back, and Sam had a sinking feeling they weren't going to budge this time. "Why is this happening to me?"

"Maybe it's been happening for some time, but you kind of missed the signs."

She pondered this. He was right. All the mishaps.

A knock on the window of the front door brought her out of her musings. She unlocked the door for Officer Andor.

"I can't get past your wards."

"Oh. Please come in Officer Andor."

The wolf stepped over the threshold. Now she knew why they couldn't enter her house.

Lucius had spelled it to exclude creatures but not humans from her dwelling. He must have suspected there were supernatural people around her. Lucius knew more than he was telling her. She'd have to grill him for answers when she had the chance.

"Want to tell me what happened?" Andor asked.

"I know Dex has probably given you his version, so I'll give you mine, and you can take down Jack's testimony too." She paused. "We were standing here in the shop and then a loud explosion sounded. We looked out and my van was on fire. How am I going to get my deliveries done now? It's the only vehicle I have."

Officer Andor stepped closer to her. "Listen Samantha, I think you're in danger and the least of your worries are your deliveries."

The bell on the door tingled and Dex walked back in. "The fire department is collecting evidence to see what type of explosion was used."

"Thanks," Andor said.

"No problem. Happy to assist."

"Samantha, this is routine and I must ask for the record. Do you know who might want to harm you?"

"For the record. No."

"I'm going to request surveillance on your house."

"You mean, police guards?"

"Yes."

She rolled her eyes. Definitely not what she needed. "Great. And what about them?" She pointed to the reporters.

"They are a problem, and now that you've had two incidents in two days, I'm sorry to say you're going to have a groupie convention out there. Don't be surprised if they park outside your house too."

Sam slapped a hand to her head. "Shoot me now."

"I'm sure somebody is trying to do just that." The lines on Jack's forehead creased.

"Not on my watch. I've had some cameras installed around your house and here at the shop. That way we can monitor any suspicious activity."

"Good idea, Dex, and something tells me whoever's behind this, they're going to send another warning," Andor said.

"Is that what you think this is, a warning?" Samantha asked. She shook her head. "Wait, you had cameras installed?

"Yes and yes."

Her mouth hung open.

"Someone wants to harm you," Dex said.

"But why go to all the trouble of killing an innocent man and torching my vehicle?"

"Because the person doing this wants you scared."

"Why?"

"Basically people who play with their targets get off on tormenting them before they move in for the kill," Dex supplied.

"Great. Now I have some whacko, sicko after me."

"Hopefully not for long," Dex comforted.

"I'll need a few more details, and I strongly suggest you go home." Andor's tone was deadly serious.

She thought about it for a moment. "No. I won't give in to some bully because that's exactly what this witch or warlock is, a bona fide bully. I've had enough. My whole life, I've been pushed and kicked..." Tears welled in her eyes, and she took a breath. "... I won't stand for it."

Dex stepped over and pulled her into his arms. "I want to know who, and I want to know when."

"There's nothing that can be done now, it's all ancient history," she said with a sob.

"I'll pop into your place later to see how you're doing," Andor said as he walked to the door.

"I might head home too," Jack added.

"You might also be a target. I'll drive you home," Andor said.

"Nah, I should be fine."

"Kid, listen to the officer." Dex's stern voice filled the room.

"Okay. I'll grab a ride with you."

They both left and Sam was still in Dex's arms. She wasn't a wilting flower, but the last two days were starting to wear her down. She put her head on Dex's chest and damn if she didn't like how it felt.

Dex considered his witch for a moment and rested his chin on her head. Whoever had treated her badly as a child would pay. He didn't need to upset or rile her up anymore. Someone was playing a dangerous game, and he would be on alert. While the firemen had put out the fire to Samantha's van, he'd organized security and another vehicle for her. He had money, and he would not wait until some human insurer decided it was a crime and not her fault.

"What is it you want to do right now?"

Sam stepped out of his embrace. "I still have to work. I have bills to pay, and the van is a major setback. Who knows when the insurance money will come through?"

He was one step ahead, and a sense of pride welled in his chest. He wasn't going to let his witch go, so she would have to slowly accept all the help he was willing to give. "You don't have to worry about that. I have arranged for a vehicle so you can continue without disruption."

Her mouth dropped open and damn if she didn't look cute.

"I can't accept that, Dex. I can't pay you for it."

"I don't want payment."

"You don't even know me that well. We're not dating."

"Well, we can fix that."

"How?"

"Go out to dinner with me." He watched for her reply and his heartbeat sped up.

"I would love that, but my life's a mess."

"Carpe Diem."

"You're right, I should. How about we have that belated lunch." She pointed to the bags of food he'd left on the counter. "That can be our preliminary date." She winked at him.

His heart did a triple somersault. She hadn't rejected him. His inner wolf rejoiced.

"After lunch, I want to tidy up."

"How about we do that first. It would be much quicker if I help."

Samantha walked to the counter, retrieved a broom and handed it to him.

"What, you're not riding this baby?" he teased.

She scoffed. "Why does everyone typecast us?"

He pulled her in with one hand. "Relax."

"I'm sorry. I'm a bit wound up." She softened her posture in his arms.

"I've got you, and I won't let anything happen to you."

"I'm starting to catch on." She let out a laugh. "Let's finish cleaning. I'm starving."

He wasn't going to argue there.

Chapter Ten

D ex didn't like to leave Samantha alone, but he had no choice. Tonight while she rested, he'd be working on narrowing down who set the bomb in her car. He had all the resources he needed at his fingertips. There were several things he wanted to check, and the first was the surveillance cameras around the street. The one he installed for Sam's shop came up empty. He knew who had to ask, and he'd already placed a call before the fire crew put out the flames.

He took the stairs two at a time and made his way to his attic office. He fired up the laptop.

His inbox had several emails waiting for him. He scoured through the ones from his ex-*Phi Athanatoi* colleagues. Two had surveillance footage and those were the ones he wanted. He watched the first. It showed people lining up to get flowers from Samantha's store. The people of Bel Haven had started to line up early in the day.

Many stood patiently, chatting amongst themselves. Nothing looked suspicious. He flipped through several hours of footage, taking in scene by scene. He watched as they arrived at the store to find Jack waiting. He saw them entering and then himself exiting the shop to control the crowd. There was nothing dubious while he kept the crowd under control, though when he went inside to check on how his witch was, a sinister figure exited from one of the shops—all clad in black.

Looked like he had a lead. The Old Timer's Music store was across the road from Bewitching Blooms. He watched the rest of the video until their mystery person placed a small bomb under Samantha's vehicle. "The nerve, and in daylight too."

In his world most of the bad came out at night, but this, this was different. He could smell it in the air. There was magic floating around, and it wasn't coming from his witch. It wasn't the warlock Lucius either. He'd gotten a good scent of him, and once Samantha explained things, he understood why he had scented him. No, this was potent, like Lucius, but with a dark edge to it. He'd need the warlock's help with this. He had an array of equipment to dull a witch or warlock's power for a few minutes, but that might not be enough time to slap on some specially made cuffs, curtesy of Phi Technologies. His ex-boss had the leading equipment to fight most creatures—that was what they did. They kept the things that went bump in the night away from humans. Kept the harmony and kept their world from being exposed.

Mankind couldn't cope with the knowledge that there were deadlier beings that lived amongst them. Those who could had experienced something other from a young age and were more likely to accept it. His ex-organization also had humans working for them and with them.

He watched the rest of the video to where the van blew up and fire engulfed it, then shut it down and made his way to his basement. He'd had Xen's organization fit it out for him just before he moved in.

He put his fingertip on the biometric pad by the door. It clicked open and he made his way down the stairs. The lights came on when he reached the bottom. He took quick steps to the locked metal cabinets lined against the walls. He put his finger on the one he wanted, and it unlocked. He stripped out of the clothes he was wearing and geared up in black combat clothing, including boots. Then he strapped on all manner of harnesses for his weapons. He moved to another cabinet that contained an array of weapons. He placed them with quick efficiency in the designated holsters. Once satisfied he made his way back up the stairs and to his garage.

He jumped into his car and hit the button on the garage door. As it rolled up, he saw Samantha standing in his driveway. She was dressed in an oversized t-shirt, jeans, and fluffy slippers. What on earth was she doing outside? He pulled out of the garage, stopped right next to her and rolled down the window. "What are you doing out here?"

"I heard a noise and thought I should check it out."

"What kind of noise?"

"The type that makes you think there's a burglar on the loose."

He switched the engine off and put the window up before getting out of the car. Best check it, and one thing was certain, the wards the warlock put up must have been working. That gave him some comfort. But Samantha out here didn't. "Let's get you back inside, and I can have a look around."

"Dex. What are you wearing?"

"I'll explain inside."

He was by her side and ushering her toward her house. The keys in her hands rattled.

"Here, let me." He took the keys from her and unlocked the front door. He swept an arm so she could enter first. Once inside he turned the lock and followed Samantha through to the living room.

She turned to him. "What's with all this?" She flicked her wrist from the top of his head to his toes and then back up again.

There were two ways this could go. One, he could skim it down completely and leave out a lot, or two, he could just tell her what his life was like and give her information as needed. His brain and inner wolf did the math. Option two was the better if he wanted to claim his mate and have a life with her.

"This is part of my ex-life. I can't give you the full story now, but what I can tell you is the main focus of the organization I worked for was to keep humanity safe from other creatures."

"When you say other creatures, do you mean witches too?" Her face dropped.

He nodded his head.

"But we don't turn into hags or anything. We just have magic or defective magic in my case."

"Yes, but the powerful witches and warlocks can do a lot of damage if left unchecked."

"And how do you as you say, keep them in check?"

"It depends. If the said witch or wizard threatens to tear open the fabric that keeps our world and the human world quiet, then we find the problem person."

"And what happens to them?"

"We ask them to come along quietly, but if they don't then we do what the police do. We cuff them and bring them in to our headquarters."

"What then?"

"We talk to them and see if we can reach some sort of agreement on why they need to tone down their magic around humans, and if they don't agree then we slap them with specific neutralizing cuffs so they can't use their magic."

"Like that would work." She scoffed.

He let out a laugh. His witch didn't know the effects on fully fledged witches and warlocks that couldn't use their magic.

He stepped closer to her. "Samantha, witches and warlocks who can't use their magic over a period of time go crazy."

Her mouth dropped open. He could see her doing the math in her head. "Is that what's happening to me, seeing as my magic is defective?"

"No, because even though your abilities are limited you still have access to the magical part of you."

"So how many witches and warlocks have you had to lock up and how many have gone crazy?"

He knew why she was asking, and he had been over the years very fortunate to have negotiated easily with other witches and warlocks. There had never been a reason to lock them up and send them to La La Land. "I've never had to lock one up yet."

"So, you think whoever is targeting me needs to be locked up?"

"I do, because I don't believe that witch or wizard is redeemable. When magical people commit crimes in the open, they are beyond salvation. There are rules Samantha, and we all have to follow them if we are to live in harmony. My ex-organization is responsible for that."

"You mean there's a whole system to keep nonhumans in order?"

"In one simple word, yes."

She nodded her head in understanding. "So whoever killed Mr. Rutherford and blew up my van will get what's coming to him or her."

"I won't lie, I won't be easy on whoever is behind it all, and I may need Lucius' help."

"I'm coming with you."

"I can't let you do that."

"Why not? You stand more of a chance of flushing out these individuals if I'm with you than if I'm sitting here."

A loud thump sounded in the backyard. Dex growled and took off toward the kitchen. His sharp sense of smell and hearing had already alerted him that there was no one else out in the backyard other than Gilbert. He had managed to get himself stuck in a small hole in the fence line between the houses. "What are you doing there?"

Gilbert whimpered.

A moment later he had Gilbert in his arms and was heading back to his witch. "Stay out of trouble little guy and look after Samantha."

His witch was standing at the threshold of the back door. "That dog is nothing but trouble."

Gilbert let out a loud yap, and Dex put him into Sam's waiting arms. She cuddled him and cooed to him.

"Get him inside," Dex said as he followed them inside and shut the door behind them. He locked the door.

"Give me a minute to settle him, and then I'm coming with you."

He didn't want her along because he didn't know what kind of danger he would face. It was too risky, but damn if his wolf didn't want her there. "Samantha, this could be dangerous."

"Dex, look at you, you are armed to the hilt."

She had a point, still he would never forgive himself if something were to happen to her. She was his, and once he took a bite from her and tasted her blood there would be no going back. Even now every fiber of his being wanted to make sure she was safe. She gave him that puppy dog look. Damn, he'd regret this. "Okay, but on one condition. You stick to me like glue. You don't wander off, and you stay behind me the whole time."

She bent and let Gilbert out of her arms before standing to her full height and did the army salute.

"Why does that make me uncomfortable?"

She shrugged. "Beats me. I'll go put my shoes on." She darted out of the room, and he listened to the soft sound of her feet up the stairs. He took in a deep breath and inhaled Samantha's scent, and gods and goddesses, if that didn't make him hard. He didn't know how much longer he could hold off. He'd have to claim her soon. His primal need for her was clouding his thoughts. He'd probably end up regretting agreeing to her coming along. He should really convince her to stay, but the other side of him wanted her around him at all times.

Soft footfalls and that sweet scent he was becoming very fond of brought him out of his musings.

"Ready when you are."

Chapter Eleven

They pulled up at the Old Timer's Music shop. Dex had explained during the drive over what he'd discovered through the footage. Her anger and rage notched up at the prospect of having had someone dangerous close by spying on her and watching her every move. It unsettled her more than she wanted to admit. How did she not know this? Why did she have to have defective powers? They got out of the car, and Dex was beside her before she could blink.

"If only I were normal."

"There is nothing wrong with you, Samantha."

"Dex, I think you didn't get the memo. I'm flawed, damaged, out of order. You know... stick a coin in, and your money gets stuck kind of broken."

He let out a deep and rumbly laugh. "Samantha, I'm sure it has a lot to do with not being given the proper training."

She thought about it for a fleeting second and it sounded good, but she knew it wasn't the reason. She had never been able to do spells like the other kids in her coven. All were functioning witches and wizards. Except for—her. "No, Dex. I don't have what other magical people have."

"You have that and more."

"How do you know that, Dex?"

He pulled her to him. "I can scent power humming in you, and this isn't a case of mistaken identity. This is the real deal."

"But... but."

He put a finger to her lips. "Wolves can scent other beings. Everyone carries their own signature, though different groups of supernatural beings have distinct scents that belong to them. Such as witches give off a creamy soda scent. Warlocks give off a cedar scent but mixed within that is their own power scent. We are able to pick up how much power that witch or warlock holds. We can also scent it long after that individual has left the area.

"So, we leave behind a signature."

"Yes."

"Did you pick it up with Lucius?"

"Yes, and I knew he was powerful, but I didn't know if he was a threat or not until I bit him. You see when I'm around you, you muddle my senses."

She swallowed hard at that admission because Dex got her all hot and twisted. "You do the same to me."

He crashed his lips to hers. She moaned in satisfaction, and he mirrored her actions. His touched every corner of her being. She shifted closer, wanting more. He obliged and there was no mistaking the effect she was having on him.

The night wind picked up, and a dog barked in the distance.

He broke the kiss. "We will continue this later."

Heat burned her cheeks, and she was sure she was glowing bright red. She tipped her head down.

He placed a finger under her chin. "Don't ever be embarrassed."

She nodded her head.

"Come on, let's go question the owner and see what his involvement is."

They walked over to the shop, which had a residence upstairs. Dex pulled out some tools.

"Are we breaking and entering?" Her voice quaked a bit. She'd never done anything so risky before.

"We sure are."

With a soft click the door eased open. Dex gave it a slight push and ushered her inside. They walked up the long narrow stairs to another door on the landing. Dex knocked on the door. There was some scratching motion from the inside before the door flung open.

"H... how did you get up here?"

"The door was open," Dex said matter-of-factly.

"What do you want?"

"We want to ask you a few questions, if you don't mind."

"Who are you, the police or somethin'?"

"No, something deadlier," Dex said, taking a step closer to Mr. Simms.

He held his hands up. "I don't want no trouble."

Samantha found her cue to bring the heat down. It was almost as if Dex knew she'd say something. "We don't either, just answer any questions we have honestly."

He nodded his head in agreement.

"I want to know who this is."

Samantha watched as Dex reached in his pocket and pulled out some photos of a darkly clad figure.

Mr. Simms' eyes went wide like saucers. He obviously recognized who the man dressed in black was. "As I said, I don't want no trouble and that there is trouble."

"A name," Dex said.

"He never gave it."

"What was he doing in your shop?"

"He walked in and basically threw two thousand dollars at me to sit in the shop and for me not to ask any questions."

"Is that the first time he approached you?"

"Yes, never seen him before. He's not from this town. We ain't that big and most folks know each other."

"Can you give us a description?" Sam asked from beside Dex.

"Round face, broken nose and a scar on his left cheek."

"Sounds like the stereotypical villain in every movie," Samantha mocked.

Dex let out a dissatisfied growl. "Give me something tangible."

"He said something about Samantha."

She stepped forward. "Spill it, what did he say?"

"That your line has to be destroyed."

Samantha scrunched up her face. "My line?"

"Yeah, you know where you come from, your parents, your grandparents and your family."

Dex stepped beside her.

"What else did he say?"

"That's it, he didn't say boo the whole time he was in here. Kept a close watch on your shop and the cops when that dead customer was found. Then the next day he was back again."

"I should strangle you." Dex growled at him. "He made it clear he wanted to harm Samantha, and you did nothing."

Mr. Simms held up his hands.

"I didn't want trouble and I'm not stupid. That man was dangerous. I'd probably be as dead as a doornail if I didn't stay silent."

Sam watched as Dex processed what Mr. Simms had said. "The police would have protected you."

"Listen, I know I made the wrong decision, and I shouldn't have taken that man's money. It gives me the shivers."

"Go to the police station and ask for Detective Nicholls and tell him everything that happened. If I were you, I'd hand in the cash too. Better to do it now before they decide you are an accessory," Dex said.

"I think Dex is right. Might be worse for you later." Samantha lifted her hand and slapped him across the arm. "For being loyal to your town folk."

"I'm sorry, Samantha. I didn't know."

"You should have backed up your own." The fact that Mr. Simms hadn't hightailed it across the street to warn her at the first signs of someone wanting to do harm to her made her throat dry up and her stomach tighten. Dex rubbed her back as if knowing what she was experiencing.

"I see that now, Samantha," Mr. Simms said.

"The damage is done, Mr. Simms. I don't think I can ever trust you."

"I'll make..." his voice cracked, "... this right, Samantha." He stepped back and held on to the entrance side table.

She wasn't an idiot, she could see the whole saga had left him shaken, confused and guilty.

"See that you do the right thing," Dex warned. "Otherwise, I'll be back."

Mr. Simms nodded his head. Samantha didn't think he'd want Dex paying him another visit.

"I'll go to the police first thing in the morning."

"Before we go, I want to look around your shop, mind letting us in?" Dex raised his eyebrow.

"Su... sure. Let me grab my keys." Mr. Simms patted himself first to check if the keys were on him then realized they were in a bowl by the front door entrance table. The three of them exited down the stairs and to the shop next door in silence.

Samantha watched as Dex looked around and up and down the street. "Get inside." He lowered his hand to the small of her back. A spark ignited in her. She liked the feel of his hand there. He leaned close to her ear. "Later," he whispered.

How did he know she was reacting to his touch?

"I can scent your change." As if being able to read her mind, he answered her question.

She turned her head to the side to half look at him. "How is that even a thing?"

"One of the perks of being a wolf."

"We need to talk."

"We do and we will."

Mr. Simms cleared his throat and pointed to the spot where their suspect had been spying on them.

Dex surveyed the area. Sam watched his actions closely. He seemed to be sniffing around the spot. *A wolf thing*, she thought. Something caught his eye, and he bent to retrieve it. A passport size notebook.

"We just hit the jackpot." Dex beamed.

Sam peered over his shoulder as he flipped through the pages. There were scattered notes throughout. Most of them in Latin. "We're going to need Lucius for this."

"I can read and understand some but not all of it and these symbols..." she pointed to one of the pages, "... I have no idea what they mean. I've never seen anything like it." Even in her training within the coven she had never come across such symbols. These looked different.

"We've got work to do." Dex closed the notebook and slipped it into his back pocket. He made his way to the door, and Sam followed without a word. Dex stopped at the threshold. "Thank you for letting us look around. Be sure to keep your promise."

Mr. Simms shuffled forward. "I will try and make this right."

Samantha wasn't a total hypocrite, she understood when cash was limited, people did what they had to do to keep their heads above water. She had hoped he would have come straight to her and warned her, but she realized no matter the last few years she'd been here, she was still an outsider to some. That thought sent a sharp spear to her chest. She had nothing more to say to Mr. Simms. She lifted her hand and gave him a wave. Life's questions rolled around in her mind as they made their way back to Dex's car.

He looked over at her after they'd buckled up. "That was more than he deserved."

It took her a second to realize what Dex meant. "I understand, but at the same time I kind of wish he'd chosen good over money."

"Human nature."

"Not everyone is like that, Dex."

"Trust me, Samantha. There are fewer who aren't."

Dex had a point.

"Can you call your warlock friend?"

She recalled Lucius had said if she needed him, all she had to do was call his name. "Uh-huh."

"Good. Let's do that when we get back to your place. I want to decipher as much as we can from that notebook. This warlock, whoever he is, is dangerous."

"I kind of worked that out."

"I know you have, but he's willing to toy with you till you're dead. I need to find him first and end this."

Samantha sat in silence for the rest of the drive, which wasn't long. Thankfully everything was close by in their small town of Bel Haven.

Once inside her house, Dex gave her a small nod to indicate his readiness. She closed her eyes and focused on Lucius then twitched her nose and called his name. "Lucius."

He appeared within a second, right beside her. She jumped as she hadn't expected him to appear immediately—in fact she'd been skeptical whether it would really work.

Dex pulled her close to him. She melted into him but didn't want to admit she loved the feel of having his strong arm around her.

"You called?"

"Well, that's obvious," Sam said, rolling her eyes.

"What can I help you with, and why does he look like he's ready for action?" Lucius waved his hand at the wolf next to her.

Dex removed his arm from around her, fished out the notebook and handed it to Lucius. "Samantha said she can read some of the Latin in that book, but I wanted you to have a look at it too. She says she's never seen the likes of these spells. What do you make of it?"

Lucius was flipping and reading through the notebook. If the look on his face was anything to go by, she'd bet those spells were not good.

"This is dark magic."

"It's what I thought but needed confirmation."

"Where did you find this?"

"This belonged to the warlock who's trying to kill Samantha." Dex folded his arms across his chest.

"These spells, they're older than old."

"What do you mean by that?" Samantha asked. "Old as in something practiced hundreds of years ago?"

"Try thousands of years ago, as in ancient."

Dex raised his eyebrow at Lucius in question, and Samantha opened her mouth to say something then shut it as her thoughts and questions cascaded in her mind.

"How far back are we talking?" Dex asked.

"Way back to Ancient Greece."

"You're joking." Sam thought it was ridiculous. She'd never heard of spells going that far back.

"I'm not," Lucius deadpanned. "These have been translated from Ancient Greek spells to Latin.

"How do you know that?" Samantha asked.

"Because this one..." Lucius pointed to a page, "... is a popular spell used by the ancient Greeks around the sixth century B.C. Usually when they wanted to curse an individual, they would write it on a lead tablet and then bury it in a cemetery, near a temple, near a theatre or in the graves of others."

Samantha let out a loud gasp. "You mean to say there's a possibility there's a curse tablet with my name on it out there somewhere?"

"Yes, possibly."

"You need to find it," Dex said before she could.

"That's the easy part. I can do a locator spell."

"If you need help, I know a powerful witch who can help." Dex knew if he asked Xen, he'd call his witch friend to assist them.

"If it's absolutely necessary then I'll ask."

"Why would someone want to do this to me?" Sam hadn't done anything to anyone and had very little to do with her coven, and now someone was after her. It just didn't make sense. She scrunched up her face.

"Your background and origins go way back. Into ancient times themselves. It makes sense then that this warlock, whoever he is, is using ancient magic to sever your line."

"What on earth did my ancestors do to this guy?"

"That's the million-dollar question," Dex said. "Do your work, warlock. I need any threat extinguished, and then we need to find this guy and I'm going to need your help."

"I have your back, wolf. Just keep her safe." Lucius lifted his chin in Samantha's direction.

"You know I'm standing here, right?"

Lucius gave her a small smile. "I need to grab a drink of water before I start."

"Help yourself," Samantha said.

He made his way through to the kitchen.

Dex turned to her. "I won't rest until this guy's lights are out. That's my vow to you."

The look on his face was pure murder, and she had no doubt the man before her would deliver on his promise.

It bothered her that she liked the thought of a strong man like Dex defending her with violence.

Chapter Twelve

Dex would not let Samantha's enemy, who was now his too, hurt a hair on her head. She was his mate and his to protect.

He had wanted to throttle Mr. Simms. If Samantha hadn't been with him, he probably would have done a lot worse. Finding the warlock's lost notebook though was pure gold. This was the lead they needed, and the sooner they unraveled the secrets within, the faster they could end any possible threat to his mate.

There was a lot riding on deciphering the notebook and working out what the warlock's next move would be.

He had just promised Sam he would kill the warlock. Never in his life had his wolf side roared and thrashed with pure blood lust. No one would harm his mate. That he almost did at her place of work was enough for Dex. He pulled her close to him.

"You are mine, and the sooner I make you mine the better."

"What does that even mean?"

"It means, go out with me tomorrow night."

"Seriously, you're asking me out on a date in the middle of mayhem."

He bent his head and gave her a soft kiss. Then coaxed her lips open and deepened the kiss. She moaned in the back of her throat, and he reciprocated then pulled back. "Say, yes."

"Yes."

"Good. I'll book something for us."

A throat cleared and Dex released Samantha.

"Ready when you two love birds are," Lucius voiced from the doorway before stepping into the living room.

"Okay, what do you need from us?" Samantha asked.

And damn if she wasn't cute and eager. Dex would never get enough of watching her.

"I need you to stand here and you over there." The warlock pointed to the far corner, showing Dex where he wanted him.

Samantha stepped closer.

"I only need you to be close. You don't need to do anything else."

Dex watched the warlock closely. He trusted him. From the moment he'd revealed he'd been watching Sam from a distance, Dex knew she was his charge. That meant he'd made a promise to her parents and to this day, he honored it. Dex respected that.

The warlock started a low chant in Latin.

Samantha's hair started to lift then subside then rose like static again. The process repeated several times as Lucius chanted. The magic around them started to swirl. On it went for several minutes. Then Lucius touched Sam on the forehead and a burst of light shot through the room. Dex squinted before locking his gaze on his mate.

She didn't seem to be fazed by any of it. "Did it work?"

"It did."

"Where is it?" Dex asked from where he still stood.

"Over in the local cemetery." Dex looked at the time, it was nearly 4 AM.

"Let's go," Sam said with all the energy she could muster.

"You're going to go upstairs and get some sleep." Dex pointed to the roof. "Lucius and I will take it from here."

"But shouldn't I be there in case you need to do something with it when you find it?"

"Dex looked over to Lucius and prayed he didn't, but luck was a funny thing, it didn't always work on your side when you wanted it to.

"We may need her," Lucius said.

Samantha grinned.

Who was he to argue with the warlock when she looked at him like that.

Dex rattled his keys.

"There's no need for that. I can get us there faster." Lucius waved a hand, and they dematerialized from Samantha's living room.

Dex hadn't had the pleasure of being transported this way before. He experienced a pulling and tearing sensation in his muscles that subsided as soon as they landed in the cemetery entrance.

Samantha didn't do so well. When they appeared, she was heaving her guts up. Dex stepped closer to help move her hair out of the way. Clearly no one had taught his witch how to dematerialize and materialize without getting sick.

When she had finished Dex tucked an arm around her. She snaked her arm around his waist for support.

He looked over to Lucius. "See that she's taught how to do that."

"On the same page, wolf."

Lucius looked at Sam with sadness. Then muttered a few expletives and her coven's name under his breath. Then something about turning them all into toads.

Dex smiled on the inside and decided he liked the warlock even more.

"Where to?" he asked, still holding on to Sam who needed a bit more time to regain some equilibrium.

"I'm sorry," she whispered.

"Don't ever apologize for being sick." He wasn't going to let his mate think she'd done something wrong.

Based on Lucius' reaction those good for nothing caretakers at her coven were to blame, and as soon as he stemmed their current target, he would make it his business to find them all and let them know what happened to witches and warlocks that get cocky. That was if Lucius didn't beat him to the punch.

"This way."

They followed Lucius as he moved through the entrance and up a rocky pathway.

"I'm okay, Dex." Samantha tugged his waist to let him know. She pushed herself away from him and fell in line with his steps.

He wasn't going to lie. He missed having her close.

"Where are we going?" Samantha asked as she followed Lucius.

"We're almost there."

The sun was starting to rise too. Dex scanned the area then checked their six to see if anyone was lurking. There were a lot of things that pointed to a very sick individual who wanted to cause harm. Dex couldn't shake the feeling this was a well laid out trap. "Why do I get the feeling we're not alone?"

"We're not. There are spirits here," Lucius said.

"What, as in you can see them?" Samantha asked.

"Feel them but if they wanted to show themselves then they already would have." Dex put his arm around her waist to guide her.

Samantha turned to Lucius. "Can you sense their presence too?"

"I can."

"I should be able to too," she whispered under her breath, but Dex heard her.

He would have to have a talk with his witch about putting herself down. He would not have her referring to herself as defective. His wolf senses told him she had power but there was something blocking her, and he intended to find out what it was, but first they had to deal with the current problem.

"Here." Lucius pointed to a grave. To say it was weathered was an understatement.

"I don't get why he chose this grave." Samantha beat Dex to the punch. His witch was in tune with his thinking, and he hadn't even mated with her... yet.

"Because it's right next to the small chapel, and that adds to the significance of it all."

"How so?" Sam asked, but Dex knew the answer to that before Lucius filled her in.

"Churches emit a certain power."

She pointed to both Lucius and him. "Do you two feel that energy too?"

Dex didn't want to disappoint his mate. Her posture and demeanor had already shifted. She cast her glance downward and her brows furrowed in contemplation. "Not exactly," he said.

He caught Lucius' eye and gave him a quick wink before Sam looked up at them both.

"How about we focus on the task, which is to dig this grave."

"You don't happen to have a shovel in that long coat of yours?" Dex asked.

Lucius waved a hand and three shovels appeared.

"Hang on. If you can wave your hand and give us these," Samantha bent to pick up one of the shovels, "then shouldn't you be able to wave a hand and have the shovels do their work on their own?"

Lucius winked at her. "You're a good witch, Samantha. Trust in yourself."

That was exactly what Dex thought.

Lucius snapped his fingers and the shovel in Samantha's hand flew forward and joined the other two shovels suspended in the air above the grave. When Lucius snapped his fingers again the shovels started moving and flinging dirt.

Dex grabbed Samantha and moved her behind him, so she wouldn't get sprayed with dirt.

Lucius snapped his fingers and the shovels sped up. After a few more loads of tossed dirt, a loud clank sounded. The digging ceased. Without a word they moved in sync toward the grave.

"Might be a good idea to use some of your warlock mojo to lift that thing," Dex said.

Lucius waved his hand and lifted the lead tablet out of the grave. It turned slowly in the air, and he stepped closer to inspect it. It buzzed with energy—magic.

Dex didn't like the looks of it, and his hackles stood on end. The tablet radiated bad, and he spun around as the air shifted. He kept Samantha behind him then reached for his gun.

Lucius reacted fast too. He threw a magical shield in front of the three of them.

The enemy had finally shown his face, and Dex wanted nothing more than to shift to wolf form and go straight for his jugular. He wouldn't move from protecting his mate though—she came first. If an opening appeared and he knew hands down what he was dealing with then he'd strike, but right now he didn't know what this guy had up his sleeve.

Lucius threw a blast of power toward the floating tablet. It started to melt before their eyes. This angered their enemy. He threw a blast of power toward Lucius. It shook his shield but didn't penetrate. Lucius fired back, and Dex decided the best spot would be in line with Lucius, so he carefully stepped back to usher Samantha backwards.

"Dex?" Samantha questioned from behind him.

"I need you closer to Lucius."

She didn't resist his actions.

The power exchange between the two warlocks amped up several notches. They were damaging other graves. The ghosts who walked here were now circling them. Dex didn't like it because he didn't have weapons for those guys. They weren't what he usually fought.

A ball of golden power hit their shield again. Each hit rattled their protection. One thing was abundantly clear to Dex, both warlocks were matched in power, which meant they could be at this all day. Dex needed to either get some answers via conversation or he put a chink in their enemy's armor. First, he'd take the social way out. He holstered his weapon then stuck his fingers between his lips and blew.

Both men stopped and looked in his direction. He raised his hands up, palms out. "This is getting nowhere. I'm opting for conversation and the need to resolve whatever seems to have ticked you off." Dex tipped his index finger toward the enemy.

He sneered. "Words don't soothe, only damage does."

"Right." Dex rolled his eyes, another one of these idiots who wanted to mess places and peoples' lives up just because they thought someone wronged them. Blame the world and everyone for everything but do nothing to fix things and move past it. He'd seen his fair share of mad men in his lifetime. The warlock before them was beyond any reconciliation and had sparked his anger toward his mate. It was anyone's guess what might have triggered his behavior because he clearly didn't want to give them the backstory as to why. Dex decided it was time for option number two. He pulled his gun out and fired it at the enemy's right foot. Weakening your enemy before taking them out was always one of his favorite tactics.

A loud yell split the air. Dex's target hit the ground and his shield dropped.

"I wasn't after you, wolf, just that no good witch behind you, but now you've made it personal." He tipped his chin toward Sam.

"Well, surprise, surprise. Now we're making progress."

Samantha stepped from behind Dex. "I don't know you and have done nothing to you."

The crazy warlock let out a laugh.

"Your line is vermin and needs to be extinguished." He sent a blast of power in Samantha's direction. Dex moved her out of the way.

Lucius intercepted, and the blast veered off and hit a tree. It toppled over.

"The minute you targeted her, you sealed your fate, warlock. This will only end one way." Dex had fought many battles in his life, and one delusional warlock was not going to scare him off. "I'll give you one chance at redemption. Leave the witch alone, and I'll go easy on you when they sentence you." He knew a proper coven would strip him of his powers if it were found he was dipping into magic he shouldn't.

Another crazy laugh split the air. "You can't hold me or try me before a coven."

"That's where you are wrong," Dex said. It was rock solid that this warlock hadn't been brought up to speed with the current magical laws.

Dex pulled out a pair of cuffs and motioned to Lucius to take down the shield. He made his way to the injured warlock. He'd torture him a bit before his conviction.

He was almost at his side when the warlock mustered enough energy through his pain to dematerialize.

"Damn." He wasn't fast enough.

"Leave it be, wolf. We'll get him. I know who he is," Lucius said from behind him.

"Spill it. I want all the details."

"In a moment." Lucius waved a hand, and all damaged headstones were replaced to their former condition. He held out his hand to Samantha, who was trying to process something, then grabbed Dex by the shoulder and they dematerialized.

They landed in Samantha's living room, and she bolted for the bathroom.

"Who's our enemy?" Dex asked Lucius.

"He went to school with Samantha's parents and me. As far as I know they were all in the same coven as kids. I have no idea what happened to him. Halfway through finishing our training he disappeared. I had very little interaction with him and never saw Sam's parents around him, so I really don't have any idea why he's targeting her."

Samantha reentered the room and stood still by Dex's side as Lucius explained who their enemy was.

"What's his name?" she asked.

"Benjamin Boggs."

Dex scoffed. "The name doesn't fit the evil warlock vibe."

Samantha let out a laugh. "No, it doesn't."

"Sometimes, warlocks and witches change their names as they come into their power."

"So does he have another name?" Samantha asked.

"*Carnifex*," Lucius answered.

"Executioner," Samantha said, translating the Latin with a smile. Her face fell a second later.

"I'm going to take a stab and say he's probably responsible for some pretty bad things."

"I knew there was someone out there by that name, riling up a lot of covens. I just didn't know it was Benjamin."

"Well, now we all do," Samantha threw in.

"What's next?"

"I need to let the covens know, but I will be back. Sam, I'll add another layer of protection to your house and workplace now that I know who our enemy is."

"Do you think my parents did something to him?"

"It's hard to say because they never paid attention to him nor did they talk to him. Everyone had their own group of friends."

"We'll get to the bottom of it. I'm sure," Dex said to reassure his mate. He pulled her to his side and wrapped an arm around her.

"The good thing is we found the curse tablet and it's destroyed. That will buy us some time before he strikes again."

"Do you think he would curse me again?"

"It's hard to say, but let's hope we're a step ahead this time. His message is clear, Sam. He wants you dead."

Samantha's posture slumped next to Dex. He tightened his grip around her. "I won't let anything happen to you."

Dex looked over to Lucius. "Warn the covens and see if we can get some assistance."

Lucius nodded in his direction and zapped out of the room.

Samantha wiggled out of Dex's embrace and turned to face him. "I really need a shower and to get ready for work."

"I know you do. Just remember I'm picking you up at seven." He tipped his head and locked lips with her.

When he was satisfied, he let her go and left her there in the middle of the living room with a big smile on her face.

That was the perfect start to the morning in his estimation.

Chapter Thirteen

S am waited for the knock on the door. She was nervous though she shouldn't have been. She'd been spending a lot of time around Dex. Yet butterflies danced in her tummy. A date. A real date and a date with her hot neighbor.

She'd listened to Dex tell her she was his over and over again.

A light tapping sounded in the vicinity of the front entrance and Gilbert barked.

"Calm down. You know who it is."

She reached for the door. When she pulled it open her she was stunned. Dex's lips turned up in amusement at her obvious reaction.

He was hot and he knew it.

"You look beautiful," he said as his eyes traveled from her face all the way down to her feet and back up again. "Green really is your color."

"This old thing." She beamed. She liked his approval, but the truth was it was an old dress. She hardly bought new things. She didn't have the time nor the social calendar that called for regular new outfits to be purchased.

"Are you ready or do you need more time?"

"Nope, I'm good to go. I'll just grab my bag."

Gilbert was yapping and Dex bent down to pick him up. He ceased when Dex cuddled him and talked to him.

"He really likes you."

Dex scratched Gilbert behind the ears. "It's a dog and wolf thing. We have an understanding."

She raised an eyebrow. "I'm not even going to ask."

Dex put Gilbert back down. He let out a whine, and Samantha bent to give him a pat.

"See you in a bit, little guy." She closed the door and stepped out into the night with Dex. She had no idea where he was taking her, and she was just going to sit back and let the night unravel. At least that was what she told herself.

"We've got a thirty-minute drive over to the next town."

They'd obviously need to fill in the time with something, so she'd use the time to find out a little more about him.

"I don't know much about you, other than that you're some ex-special ops wolf."

He let out a laugh. "I guess that's a good way to put it, and there's not much to know.

I've been around for a while, and I have a lot of loyal friends. I'm an Alpha wolf to a small pack just a few towns over. I chose Bel Haven as my place to retire."

"Retire? You don't look a day over thirty." She laughed.

"Good genes." He winked.

"No seriously, how old are you?"

"Give or take, about one hundred and thirty-two."

Her mouth dropped open. She shook her head. She must not have heard him right. "Did you say thirty-two?"

"Yes, plus one hundred."

"You're joking."

He turned his head and looked at her.

"Witch's brew, you're serious. You've been around that long?"

He nodded his head slowly.

"Does that make you like a sleazy grandpa or something?"

"No, Samantha. For wolf years I'm actually quite young."

She never thought much about age other than the years she'd lived with her coven and on her own, but she did know witches and warlocks lived long lives. Up to now she didn't think that was applicable to her because she was defective, and she never allowed herself to dwell on it.

"Any siblings?"

"Nope, only child. My parents moved to Maine quite some time ago."

"When's the last time you saw them?"

"Just before I moved to Bel Haven. I stayed with them for a month before coming out here."

She pondered what he said. He was obviously close to his parents. "Why not stay near them? Why here?"

"To be honest, I don't know. I felt a pull and wanted to come. We used to visit here years ago because I had an elderly aunt who lived here."

"Does she have family here?"

"No, they moved to the big city ages ago."

"Did you want to be on your own?"

"Yes and no but when I moved in, I realized it was fate that had intervened."

"How so?"

"Look at me, Sam."

It was the first time he'd called her that—she turned her head.

"You are my mate. I knew it the second I scented you."

She swallowed hard. He was dead serious, and the various lights on the dashboard of the vehicle further highlighted his steely demeanor. He wasn't kidding about this mate stuff. "Can you at least explain."

"A wolf only mates once in his entire life. The bond between a wolf and mated partner is strong. It allows the wolf to tap into their mate more strongly."

"How so?"

"They are both connected on an ESP level, in that the wolf can sense if their partner is in any danger or any form of distress."

Dex slowed down and took a turn off the main road. A minute later they came to a stop at a nice riverside restaurant.

"So, you're saying with this mating thing you'd be able to receive a text message from me to your brain that says help."

"That and more."

He unbuckled his seatbelt, dashed around to her side and opened the door. He held out his hand and she slid hers in his. When his fingers closed around hers, a sharp jolt danced between them. He pulled her up and into his arms.

"When we mate, and we will, I'll be able to sense more than when you need help. I'll be able to sense your need for me. Now we're not mated, but I can scent and sense your need."

His lips met hers fiercely, his tongue seeking hers. She granted him entrance without any fight. They were both equally attracted to each other. She moaned into his kiss, and he reciprocated and pulled her a little tighter. One of his hands traveled down to her ass. He gave her a squeeze and pushed her into his hardness. There was no mistaking how much he wanted her. Her mind had turned to mush, and her body hummed with anticipation. Her nipples tightened and felt restricted in their confinement. She grew wetter with each stroke of his tongue, and her pussy pulsed with need.

He broke the kiss, released her from their embrace, threaded his fingers through hers and tugged her toward the entrance of the restaurant with a huge grin on his face.

Her mind took a second to catch up and when it did one thing was crystal clear. Dex would be the kind of man who took charge in the bedroom. Another wave of heat washed through her, and she tingled all over.

Once inside, Dex gave his name for the reservation, and they were taken to another part of the busy restaurant where it was quiet. He helped her into her seat and leaned down from behind her. "I swear to you, you will only feel bliss when I make you mine." His words were thick with promise.

Heat and need washed through her like a tsunami. Her body reacted in a way she had never experienced with other men and what fleeting short exploits she'd had thus far been exposed to.

They got through dinner with more easy conversation, and when it came to dessert, Dex asked, "Would you like it here or to go?"

She looked at the waiter. "We'll have it to go."

They waited a few minutes while their chosen desserts were packaged up. When the waiter dropped their sweets on the table and gave them the check, Dex paid and ushered her to the car. He opened the door for her. When he got inside, he leaned over and gave her a chaste kiss.

"Your place or mine?" he asked.

"Mine." She knew what was coming, and her body thrummed with need.

He let out a low rumble. Then sniffed the air. "I can scent your arousal. I'm doing everything in my power not to pull over and take you."

"Okay, let's talk about what's been happening."

"That's a good idea. I'd rather a soft bed than the car."

"Me too." She agreed because she'd had car sex before, and it was not all it was cracked up to be. Most uncomfortable of places. "What do you make of all of this?"

"Ben's personal witch hunt?"

"Yes. What do you think triggered it?"

"Hard to say, and I've dealt with other maniacs over the years. It's usually something like revenge for being cast out or neglected."

She thought about that and wondered how many orphan children out there probably experienced similar emotions of revenge for being abandoned. She remembered her own circumstances and her anger at everyone for not having her parents. "You think that's what's driving his hate?"

"Hard to say," Dex answered.

They continued their conversation, and Dex was a wealth of information. He had experienced so much, and it gave her food for thought.

He pulled up to her driveway, and she rummaged through her bag for the garage remote. Dex rolled the car inside.

Gilbert was happy to see them. He started yapping as soon as they entered the house.

"Calm down." Sam gave him some water and a snack.

Once he was settled, she led them both upstairs and closed the door.

"Sam, I want you, and I won't be satisfied until my cock is buried to the hilt in your pussy."

Warmth rose to her cheeks. "That's a bit forward." Her brain and body liked his dirty mouth.

"I don't mince words when it comes to how I feel. Especially with you." He stepped forward and wrapped an arm around her waist. "If you don't want this, say so now because if I start, I won't stop."

"I want you," she whispered.

He peeled or rather ripped the shirt from his body. Then removed his pants and socks in seconds. She gazed upon all that hard thick muscle and was awestruck.

"I take it you approve?" The cocky wolf grinned, standing there in his underwear.

She nodded her head. Her fingers made quick work of pulling her zipper down and releasing her dress. It pooled at her feet, revealing the see-through underwear she'd chosen at the last minute. She was glad she had.

"Minx, I'm going to take my sweet time with you."

He stepped forward and bent his head to her breasts. He put one hand on one and squeezed and pinched her nipple then put his mouth on the other over the material and sucked hard.

She felt liquid seep onto her underwear.

He took a sniff of the air and growled. "Your scent is killing me." He dropped to his knees. "Spread your legs."

She did as he asked.

He ran a finger along the seam of her pussy. "So wet."

She wanted him. "Dex."

He buried his head between her legs and his tongue found her wet center. He moved the G-string to the side and started his ministrations, moaning as he went.

That fueled her own passion, and she moaned in appreciation of the attention she was receiving.

Her hips started to move. He pulled her panties down slowly, all while still giving her the attention she needed and wanted.

She wanted to reciprocate and get her mouth on him. "Dex."

"Hmmm."

He kept his strokes even, building his pace. The sight of Dex on his knees fueled her fire. She wouldn't last long. She broke apart and splintered with her orgasm. She was boneless. He lowered her to the bed.

Dex got to his feet and pulled down his underwear.

She took in his thick, long cock.

"Spread your legs for me."

She did as he requested.

He lowered himself to her entrance and languidly slid in.

She greedily took all of him. When he started to move, she did too.

He reached down to her bra and ripped it off. Her breasts spilled out. He palmed them, and she loved the feel of his hands on them.

"I wanted this from the moment I scented you. You are mine."

"I wanted the same."

He continued pumping into her. He leaned forward, and she ran her hands over his chest. He moaned his approval.

He reached forward and pinched her nipples as his rhythm started to build, and she shattered for a second time.

"Are you on birth control?"

"Yes."

"I'm going to mate with you."

"I want that."

"He leaned forward and bit near her shoulder."

She shattered again, and he filled her with stream after stream of his seed.

He collapsed on her, kissing her all over her face. Then he pulled out and went to the bathroom to get a cloth to clean her up.

Dex snuggled into bed with her, and her eyes fluttered a few times before becoming heavy and dragging her to sleep.

Chapter Fourteen

"Now repeat after me. *Huc*."

Sam twitched her nose. "*Huc*."

The broom flew from the back of the room and hovered near her, then dropped.

"Well, that's better." Lucius' eyebrows had turned inward.

Samantha got the feeling he wasn't impressed with her. They'd practiced and practiced, and although the spells were better, none of them actually worked the way Lucius' did. Even though it was the same spell.

"You're blocking yourself. You have convinced yourself you are no good. That's why the spell dissipates."

"It wears off? That's why it doesn't work?" she asked.

"Exactly." Lucius waved his hand, and the broom returned to its proper place. "Now try that again, but this time I want you to believe you are the best witch on the planet and that broom belongs in your hand."

She tried to muster all the self-belief she could. She was the best, she told that stupid brain of hers. Her spells worked just like Lucius' did and just like he said.

She twitched her nose and held out her hand. "*Huc.*"

The broom appeared in her hand. She closed her fingers around it.

Clapping sounded in the room. "Brava." Happiness beamed on Lucius' face.

"I can't believe that worked."

"There's the keyword. Believe." Lucius snapped his fingers, and the broom was gone. "Belief is important. Magic is nothing without belief. You have this power, Sam, you can use it if you believe."

"So, all my accidents?"

"Happened because your magic would just fizzle out halfway, and it did so because you didn't think it would work."

"You're saying I could have avoided half of that."

Lucius nodded.

She'd been a fool, and nobody had bothered to tell her. "I needed your help and wisdom a long time ago." Someone to nurture her and to help her understand her powers.

"You did, and I have dealt with your coven and the people who were responsible for passing that wisdom down to you."

"Should I be worried when you say, dealt with?"

"No. They have admitted to their lack of teaching."

Her heart swelled a bit that Lucius had stepped in, even if it was late. "Thank you."

"There is no need for thanks. I should not have fully trusted that they would do their job. I should have checked in. I failed you."

"No, you didn't. They did. You did what you understood to be the proper thing by placing me there to be trained. As most magical children are." She wasn't going to blame Lucius—it had been her coven's responsibility to see she was trained.

"Okay. Let's try a few more times to see if you have the hang of it."

She prepped herself again. This time she truly believed she could blitz magic where she wanted, and things would go as she wished. She imagined the broom was in her hand but also that the store was neat and not the mess it had been in when Lucius appeared to start training her. In her mind's eye she imagined she was perfect with her magic like all the students from her coven. "*Huc*," she whispered, twitching her nose three times.

The broom appeared in her hand without hovering, and the shop was instantly transformed into a tidy space. She let out a deep belly laugh full of joy.

Lucius grabbed her and gave her a huge hug. His laughter filled the shop. "That's what I'm talking about."

"I can't believe I did that."

"Believe. Because you did, and you did more than place the broom in your hand. You cleared the room with just one spell. You have strong magic in you, Samantha."

The bell on the shop door rang. Dex walked in. "What's the cause of celebration?"

"Samantha just executed the perfect spell. I think with practice she'll be a natural in no time."

"Once we discover what has been suppressing her power, I think we will all be surprised," Lucius said.

There was that. She had a crazy warlock trying to curse her. Who could do that and why? A rock formed in her belly. People were out to get her, and she had no idea what significance she played in anything. She was a defective witch after all, and she'd done nothing to warrant such behavior.

"Sam, none of this is your fault." Dex stepped closer to her. These guys are lunatics, and you are not to blame for their issues."

"Dex is right, Sam. Nothing you did is cause enough for this. Ben or Benjamin has a screw loose. We've heard the whisperings of this so-called executioner. Trust me, a lot of those rumors are demented and overinflated. Hard to believe that Ben is a lethal killer. He's dangerous though and don't forget that. Why he targeted you is beyond me."

Then it hit her like a two-by-four across the head, and a sharp sensation stabbed her like a spear in the chest. "Do you think crazy Ben had anything to do with my parents' disappearance?"

Lucius looked her square in the eyes. "I've suspected as much from the moment Ben appeared at the graveyard." He dropped his gaze to the floor. He was contemplating something, and Sam wanted to know what.

"Spit it out, warlock. We're all working together here, and if you have some information we can all use, now is the time to share it." Dex didn't mince his words, and that was something Samantha was starting to admire about the man. He was a no-nonsense guy.

"When your parents disappeared, I found a ripped piece of material with the old coven's logo on it, and we all assumed it may have been your father's or mother's and it somehow got torn off. Lots of coven who graduated at that time still wore the coven's logoed t-shirts around the house."

Dex shifted from his position. "You guys never sent it in to forensics, did you?"

Lucius' face fell to a frown and regret stole across his features for a blink of a moment. He shook his head from side to side in admission of their lack of proper investigation.

"I don't know why they didn't. The guy leading the case then has since passed away."

"You..." Dex pointed at Lucius, "... need to go back to your coven and open that case up. If that piece of evidence belongs to the so-called executioner, then he's more than likely responsible for Sam's missing parents."

"You don't think he killed them?" Sam had a bone-deep feeling that even though she asked that question, she knew Ben was somehow responsible.

"I'm not going to lie. There's every possibility he may have had something to do with it."

"Why did he spare me then, only to come back and kill me now?"

"It's hard to know why killers act a certain way," Dex said. "Some clarification on that piece of evidence might help us understand what happened." He pulled out his phone and fired off a message to someone before pocketing it again. "Warlock, get me that evidence, and I'll personally see it's processed."

"I'll talk to the coven about reopening this up." Lucius waved a hand and disappeared.

Dex turned to Samantha and pulled her in. He planted a chaste kiss on her lips. "Why didn't you tell me about what happened to your parents?"

"You never asked."

"We both shared at dinner last night. I need to know everything, Sam. I can't help if I don't."

"Well, it's not something I can blurt out." She lowered her gaze to his chest. That wide, strong chest.

He stuck a finger under her chin. "I know it hurts, I can feel it from you. Your hurt is my hurt."

"I don't want you hurting for me."

"Too late, it's part of the package deal." He smiled down at her.

The bell on the door rang, and the door swung open. Tom, the barber, from across the road came rushing in. "Sam."

Dex let her go, and she turned to see what had him riled up. "S-s-sam," he stuttered. He never did that.

She walked toward him. "What's the matter?"

"A man came into my shop moments ago and said to give you this." He held out a note with a shaky hand. "He said it was a matter of life or death."

Dex moved to Sam's side, and she held her hand out to receive the note.

Someone had cut out letters from a magazine and pasted *Mistwel* and *Nine O'clock tonight*. A three-hour drive from Bel Haven. Sam couldn't help but scrunch up her face.

"Real professional right there," Dex commented on the pasted words. "Who gave you the note?"

The bell to the shop rang again and Detective Nicholls and Officer Andor walked in.

"Talk about timing," Sam said, looking up from the life or death, as Tom put it, message.

"What seems to be the problem?" Detective Nicholls asked.

Sam opened her mouth.

"We were just given a note from Tom," Dex said, lifting his chin toward the said man.

She closed her mouth and gave him a sideward glance. He grinned at her.

"Wait a minute." Andor pulled some thin gloves from one of his pockets. He snapped one on before taking the note from her hand. A small smile tugged at his lips. "In what day and age does the person who handed this to you think they are in?"

Sam lifted her shoulders. "No idea but..."

Nicholls turned to Tom. "Who handed you the note?"

"I can't tell you because he was wearing a helmet and bike gear. Just came in and handed it to me and said it was urgent and that I needed to bring it over to you."

"Thank you, Tom. You can go. I can see a line outside your shop door."

"Thank you, Detective." Tom rattled his shop keys.

"See you, Sam, and you must be the new fellow in town."

"Dex." He held out his hand to Tom.

"Pleased to meet you. Take care of Sam. She's a good girl." He winked in her direction.

"Thanks, Tom. I appreciate you dropping that off." He'd been the most welcoming shop owner on the street when she moved in.

"Not at all, Sam. I don't know what trouble you're in, but please be careful."

She waved her hand around to the other men in the room. "I have these guys."

"And I'm glad." He walked to the door and let himself out.

"What do you make of it?" Dex said to Andor.

Andor lifted the page and sniffed it. "There's a faint scent on the page—female."

"Great, more people who want me dead."

Nicholls lifted a hand to her. "We won't let anything happen to you, Samantha."

"I appreciate it, though I can't ask you to look after me every second of the day. You have enough duties to attend to."

"That's true but our duties go beyond the human world. There's some serious stuff going down, and we have to assist Dex in cleaning it up. The less human attention we get the better."

"We actually came in to tell you the coroner has ruled the death of Mr. Rutherford was not natural."

Sam's eyes widened. "What does this mean?"

"It means we're rounding up any possible suspects," Andor said.

Nicholls nodded his head in agreement.

"You're not putting me on that list, are you?"

"No, Sam. You have a solid alibi," Nicholls said.

"Someone came forward to vouch that you were seen at home around the time Mr. Rutherford was murdered." Andor raised an eyebrow and looked at Dex.

"Wait. What?" She turned to Dex. "You said I was home?"

"Well, you were." His lips quirked up and a flash of images cascaded through her mind. Heat rose to her cheeks.

Andor cleared his throat. "So, you have a solid alibi and it's on record."

She shook the images of a topless Dex out of her mind. "We all know it was crazy Ben who killed him. Same with the burning of my van."

"Crazy Ben?" Both Andor and Nicholls repeated at the same time.

"I'll fill you in later," Dex said.

They nodded.

"So, backpedaling a bit in our conversation here. From the human side of things we need to treat it like a human murder," Andor filled in.

"But what will happen when there are no human suspects, which we know there won't be?"

"Sadly, it becomes another one of those cold cases," Nicholls supplied.

Her brows knitted together. "Then we owe it to Mr. Rutherford to take down Benjamin."

"I couldn't agree more," Dex said.

"Now what do we do with that?" Sam pointed to the note still in Andor's hand. "The messenger said it was life or death."

"It smells like a trap, Sam," Dex answered.

"One hundred percent, but we know better," Nicholls said.

"What do you propose we do?"

"We're going to play along, but we'll run our own reconnaissance and be prepared," Dex said to Nicholls and Andor.

"Want us to organize that?"

"I do."

"What are we up against?" Andor asked.

"A demented warlock with a heavy dose of power. We might need to gear up for this."

Both men looked at Dex. He was giving the orders.

"We'll take the note, Sam," Andor said.

She just nodded.

Both men left without another word.

"Dex, those men are the police and were taking orders from you."

"Because in the nonhuman world, I'm their Alpha."

"What exactly does that mean?"

"Wolves have a pack ranking. The Alpha is responsible for the whole pack."

She nodded in understanding.

Whatever was coming, she was sure of one thing. They needed weapons.

"You wouldn't happen to be able to loan me some of your fancy weapons?"

Dex let out a laugh.

Chapter Fifteen

Dex led Samantha to a door. He placed his finger on the biometric pad. Clicking gears sounded as it unlocked. He pulled it open to reveal stairs that descended into darkness. He took the first step down, and the lights came on automatically.

Samantha had a bad feeling about this trip to Mistwel.

"It's definitely a trap, Dex. I'm sure it is."

"It is, and I'm not gonna lie about it, but we have to go on the off chance we can finish this. I won't have that lunatic warlock roaming around. He's a menace as much as he is dangerous."

"Yes, but he's also cunning."

"That's why we're going to take some reinforcements with us." Dex wiggled his eyebrows and grinned at her. "Plus, lots of amo."

They had reached the bottom of the stairs. Sam took a look around the room. The space resembled a military supply room.

Black cages lined part of the wall space.

"Dex, all you need is an army."

"Don't worry. I can always get one of those with a few phone calls."

She was sure there wasn't even a hint of a lie in that statement. "I'm sure you can," she deadpanned.

"Listen, we don't know what that crazy warlock is going to throw at us. I want you geared up too." Dex walked toward a cupboard.

When he opened it, all manner of black gear hung inside. He pulled a t-shirt out and some pants. He handed them to her.

"Dex, these won't be my size."

He raised an eyebrow. "Trust me, they'll fit. Come here."

She followed him, and he opened another cupboard that housed several black boots and right next to the big pair of boots were smaller ones.

"You have women's sizes here too?"

"I do."

"Why?"

"Because there are women in my old organization and sometimes, like now, there may be a situation."

"I thought you retired."

"I did, but I wasn't going to take any chances. This was more to lend support to any men or women needing to reload for an assignment. Plus, the thought of being weaponless didn't sit well with me. It's just a few supplies."

"Weaponless, a few supplies," she repeated and let out a laugh. "In this room that's a vast understatement."

He laughed deeply and it sounded sexy.

"Careful, Sam, if you start thinking like that, I won't be responsible for making us late."

Heat rushed to her cheeks.

"Don't be embarrassed. I'd like nothing more than to take my sweet time with you."

"But we have bigger fish to fry right now."

"We do."

He handed her a pair of boots then motioned for her to follow. He led her to a smaller room that was a changing room. "Put that stuff on, and I'll get you some weapons."

She nodded and commenced undressing. A small growl escaped Dex's lips when he got sight of her bra. She smiled inwardly, loving that she could elicit that kind of behavior from him. In that moment she felt the need to pinch herself that Dex was hers. A bubble of joy danced in her chest.

"I feel the same," Dex shouted from beyond the room.

She'd have to get used to this mating connection they had. It was all so very new, and having Dex attuned to her own emotions was not something she was used to.

"It will take time," Dex said as he reappeared with an armload of weapons. "I'm going to give you a set of these cuffs just in case he gets near. If he does, I strongly advise you to get up close and personal so you can at least hook one of these cuffs on his wrist.

That will neuter his power. It will give me a chance to disarm him completely."

Sam nodded in understanding as Dex wrapped a belt around her waist and secured the cuffs in a leather pouch. "What if he has other warlocks there?"

"That's a possibility, and I'm counting on it. I need a good dust-up. Haven't had one in a while. Which brings me to this." He showed her a silver gun. It looked like a regular gun. Not that she had any experience with these things but from what she saw on television.

"This is a stun gun. It has a dart with witch's poison laced inside it."

"Witches' poison?" she questioned.

He smirked. "One of the witches at my previous place of employment helped formulate special darts for slowing magical people down."

Sam's brows knitted together.

"It doesn't kill them."

"Why was there a need for this?"

"Because we realized no matter how well trained we were, we were powerless against some magic users. Trust me, most are usually okay, but there are exceptions, like Ben."

"Yes, there are."

"You aim this at him or anyone else and you fire. It will do what the cuffs do but for a shorter amount of time."

She nodded her head. "Who else will accompany us?"

"We've got Nicholls, Andor and Lucius."

She processed that silently, wondering what lay ahead. How had the perfect reinvention of her life turned into something out of a thriller on TV. "Seriously, Dex, I want nothing more than to end all this drama and go back to my normal boring life."

"Trust me, Sam, everything will return to normal, for a while that is."

"What does that mean?"

"Think about it. You're a witch, I'm a wolf. What do you think our children will be like?"

She was sure the color had drained from her face. She'd never thought about being a mom. Did this gorgeous man want to have babies with her? He girly parts did a little dance, and her excited pulse thrummed between her legs.

"You keep thinking whatever it is you're thinking, and I'll strip you right here, right now."

That sounded like a better idea than a long drive into another town that looked like a TRAP in capital letters.

"Sam, we need to put a stop to this guy. I can't have him running around trying to harm my mate."

She'd have to talk to him more about this mating business, but not now. He was right, they had to resolve this. "I'm ready."

"That's my witch." He winked.

And she really liked the way he threw in the "my."

The shrill of a phone sounded in the underground space. Dex answered. "We're ready. I'll meet you both in the town's center." He ended the call and slid the phone in his pocket.

He collected a few more things and added them to a duffel bag. Then he handed Sam what appeared to be a bulletproof vest.

"What's that for?"

"What it's normally for."

"You think they'll bring guns to the fight?" she asked, trying for a bit of humor."

"I'm sure they will bring their version—magic." He winked.

"In that case let's get this baby on too. No such thing as being too armed."

Dex helped her before grabbing all the gear and heading back up the stairs and to his SUV. He made quick work of loading everything up and getting them on the road to their destination or death.

"Samantha, we have a backup plan. Andor will get you out of there if things go the other way."

"That doesn't give me comfort. What happens to you?"

"You do realize I've been around for quite many years, and I've been doing this kind of thing with all sorts of monsters?"

She swallowed hard. There were things out there she'd thought were only stories, all meant to scare them as kids. She was even sitting next to one of those stories. "What other kinds of creatures are out there?"

"Most of what you've been taught, and maybe a bit more."

"Like?" She gave him a side glance then averted her eyes back to the road.

"Vampires, demons, sirens, demi-gods, gods."

"Wait, you're saying there are gods?"

He turned to her. "Yes."

A heaviness settled on her chest. The enormity of knowing all mythical creatures and gods actually existed was too much for her brain. That changed everything, didn't it? She was sure in her mind it did. "Dex..." She trailed off.

"Don't stress about it. We have lots of time to talk about all these things, and, hey, I'll even introduce you to some of these other creatures. They're not all bad. Remember that's what I did before. There's a whole organization that polices those things."

"What would humankind think if they knew?"

"That's why there are others working hard on this to make sure they never know. It would cause chaos, and you know humans are frail and would not stand a chance if there was an all-out us against them war."

Dex had a point, and she wasn't going to argue. She sat most of the way, contemplating her past, present and future. Dex was in sync with her.

"Don't stress about what you don't have control over. We'll face what's ahead together." He took one hand from the steering wheel and squeezed hers.

She liked the feel and the warmth of it. It gave her a level of comfort. She was no longer alone.

"Just promise me one thing, Sam."

"Anything."

"If you need to use your magic, then do it."

"But it's useless."

"No, it's not. From what I saw when you were with Lucius—well, that gives me some confidence you have it in you."

He was partially right. She'd managed to get the broom to her and clear the room. She would have to keep that in mind and remind herself if needed.

They talked more about random things, and that chewed up time. She loved listening to Dex's laugh. When had she ever had something like this? Never, because none of the past encounters were right. Dex was right in all the ways she imagined. A little bubble of joy danced in her chest. If only they weren't on their way to a certain doom-and-boom. Lots of things were going to go boom. Hopefully they would survive.

They pulled into town fifteen minutes after Nicholls and Andor. They then followed the officers outside the main area of town to a less public space—a small diner.

They all headed in and sat at a booth. Sam looked around her. It was pretty dead, save for the old guy in the back nursing a cup of coffee and scribbling something down on a piece of paper.

"How do we know where they want us to go?"

"We don't. We've got a team doing some ground investigation and have tapped into the Phi Technologies team's surveillance cameras. They can only hide under a cloak for so long. It's amazing what you can pick up today," Andor said.

"How long before we have some verification of activity?" Dex asked.

"Should be a few minutes. So far the main town is clear, and we want to keep it that way."

Nicholls and Andor's phones beeped. They read their messages.

"Looks like we've got a lock on location," Nicholls said.

"Where?" Dex asked.

"The woods."

"Of course that's where they are."

Chapter Sixteen

Dex's team had zeroed in on some witchy activity in a dense wooded area outside of town. "I was thinking the note Tom gave us could have been more specific. Don't you think?"

"They wanted us exposed and ina public space. That's why they directed us here. We can't risk exposure, nor let any innocents get harmed," Dex answered.

"Do you think they want exposure?"

"Hard to say when you have a lunatic leader and followers who would agree to anything he wants."

"Fanatics."

"Exactly," Nicholls said, unloading some gear from his vehicle.

Dex fished out his phone from his pocket and typed a message. That was the third time she'd seen him do that since arriving in town.

"Lucius?" she questioned.

He looked up to her. "Yes, possibly held up. I've given him the location. I'm sure he can zap himself here a lot faster than it took us."

"That's a certainty." She remembered how sick she'd been when Lucius had materialized them to the graveyard. She wasn't keen on doing that again just yet.

"How many men have you?" Dex asked Nicholls.

"I have three men positioned just outside their circle gathering."

"A ritual?" Sam said.

"It's what it looks like."

"But for what? There's nothing specific about tonight."

"Usually the covens participate in ritual activity around the solstice and equinox."

"And there's usually no cause to watch over them," Dex said. "But tonight is something other."

"How do you want this to play out, Dex?" Andor asked.

"I want Sam with you, Andor, and nowhere near the circle."

"If any of you find yourselves close to the circle, throw a smoke bomb and get out. There's bound to be some hostility. That crazy warlock won't play fair. I've seen the power he can wield. I'm counting on Lucius." Sam watched as Dex pulled out his phone again and sent another message. He waited a second then re-pocketed it.

Dex stepped closer to Sam and put a small button receiver in her ear. "So you can hear what's going on. If you want to say something just tap it."

She lifted her hand and did a test. "I think I've got it," she said.

He pulled her to him and gave her a deep ,open-mouthed kiss that promised more. She was sure he would deliver when they got out of their current situation.

"Okay, let's move out."

Andor motioned for Sam to follow him. They took off to the left and Dex and Nicholls to the right.

"Not my idea of late-night activity."

"No, it's not." Andor chuckled. "From here on in, we are going to have to be as quiet as mice."

"Got it." Of course they had to. They were sneaking up on a gathering. There'd be no element of surprise if she was yakking away.

She followed Andor with careful steps. Lucky he had his night vision goggles on. Her eyes had somewhat adjusted to the darkness, and she couldn't shake the heavy rock that had formed in her belly and refused to shift. Whatever was going to happen here tonight, it wasn't going to be good. If the cemetery was a taste of what Ben could throw at them then she hated to think what he would do with a few extra witches and warlocks on his side. Still, she had done nothing to the man, but his hatred for her was irrefutable.

151

It was her or him, and something told her she would not go out without a fight. Wasn't that what she'd been doing from a young age? Fighting with her coven, fighting to stay ahead? If only she could have wielded half the power that most of the magical people in her community could.

Andor stuck a hand out and motioned for her to stop. She did as signaled. Then he raised a finger to his lips to denote she should stay quiet. She nodded in understanding. He then made some signs that said stay put. Again, she indicated she would. Andor fished something from his belt. He handed her a pair of night vision goggles, assisted her in putting them on and stepped a few feet forward. Taking his position toward some faint voices.

She mimicked him.

She could make out movement. There were three people deep in conversation, or so it seemed from her spot.

Andor motioned for her to follow.

She concentrated on making her steps soft. Something tickled her nose. Oh no, she was going to give them away. She waved her hand around, trying to diffuse the sneeze.

She twitched her nose. A flare of light shot up into the night sky. Her stomach rolled and chills spread over her whole body. Her magic announced their location. "Stupid defective magic."

Andor turned to look at her and all hell broke loose.

"There's someone out there," she heard one of the witches warn.

Andor grabbed her by the hand. "Way to go, Sam."

"Honestly, it was an accident. I didn't mean to do it. It's doofus magic."

A blast of power zoomed by them, and Andor pulled her to the ground. She spat out dirt and leaves.

A howl sounded in the distance. "Is that?"

"Shh. Yes, Nicholl's probably shifted to get to the witches." Andor directed her to move slowly, and she followed on her hands and knees. They had just circled into position when another strong blast of power shot up into the air.

"The witches calling for help," Andor whispered. "We best give the boys some backup while we still can."

From their position the witches had their backs to them.

Andor let loose a round of disarming bullets, which were more like darts. These would null the witches' powers and give them enough time to put the special cuffs on them. His aims hit the first two witches. Nicholls pounced a second later and dug his fangs in the leg of one witch.

She screamed.

Dex came out of the thicket of trees and slapped some nulling cuffs on one witch. The third witch took off running, yelling a spell. A second later Ben appeared.

Sam and Andor watched from their position.

Dex had moved outside the circle and so had Nicholls in his wolf form.

Ben blasted them with power, and they were propelled backward. He was about to throw more power when Sam twitched her nose and held her hand up. "*Scutum*," she whispered.

The power Ben threw bounced back in his direction. He scrambled from his position and regained his footing before throwing multiple balls of power back in Dex and Nicholl's position. It hit the shield and vibrated.

The shield would not hold for much longer.

"*Retro*." A silent wave of power vibrated through the air and pushed Ben backward. Shock and surprise marred his features.

Sam did a small dance on the inside.

This gave Dex and Nicholls the time they needed.

"Come out, come out, little witch."

Ben took a three hundred and sixty degree turn. "I know you're here and my, my, who's been teaching you some tricks?"

She thought of Lucius and his faith in her. The air around her shifted, and Lucius stood next to her. "Need some help?"

"You bet," Andor said.

Lucius threw several balls of power toward Ben who had called for reinforcements. Sam was surprised to see a couple of witches from her old coven. She didn't know them personally but knew who they were. "The nerve, siding with that nut job."

The witches were relentless. Dex managed to get two more but as soon as those were out of action two more would replace them.

"Where are they getting more recruits from?" Andor asked.

"Looks like it's more than one coven," Nicholls supplied.

"We can't get close. There are too many of them."

Dex pulled out another gun from his holster. "Shoot to wound," he said. He fired several shots, and two witches went down. Blood poured from their wounds to their legs. The witches he hit squealed in pain, and several others grabbed the injured and disappeared. Ben saw what was going on and fired a blast of power in their direction.

Dex threw Sam to the ground and covered her. Several more blasts of power hit near them.

Lucius found a gap and blasted Ben. This shot him straight up in the air. He managed to bring himself down without any harm then chanted something she couldn't make out and directed it to Lucius. The warlock countered it and the impact hit the thick line of trees.

Ben changed his target direction and aimed it to where Sam, Dex, Andor and Nicholls were shooting. They hit their targets with precision, injuring several witches. The action slowed and the witches stopped appearing out of nowhere.

Ben's pulsing power hit, sending them all propelling through the air.

They landed with a hard thud. Ben threw another surge of power in Sam's direction. She saw it and closed her eyes. She heard a loud growl—Dex.

She twitched her nose and thought of bright, powerful white light. She held out her hand to block the power. It didn't hit. It dissipated.

Lucius threw a ball of red power in Ben's direction He was surprised by her action and didn't see it coming. It hit him in the chest, propelled him backwards and he disappeared midair.

The only one remaining was the cuffed witch yelling that she would be avenged. "You'll pay."

"Heard that one before," Sam deadpanned.

"Come on, old gal. Your backup singers are out of town."

"You'll pay."

"Can someone gag her? Lucius said.

Sam raised an eyebrow.

"What? I'm sure you don't all want to hear that on replay."

"Point made," Nicholls said.

They dragged her to her feet and loaded her up in the SUV.

"Let's get you two to a secure location," Nicholls said.

"I'll leave you to it," Lucius said. "I need to warn the covens." He waved a hand and disappeared.

Chapter Seventeen

Andor and Nicholls dropped a few bags on the kitchen counter.

"We're going to make our way back into town. We've got two other men who will take the witch we have into custody over to a facility in the next town."

"What will happen to her?"

"We'll question her and then her coven will deliver her punishment," Dex said.

Samantha wondered whether they would strip her of her power. She had heard gossip when she was young. Right now though, she was tired. She stifled a yawn.

"I think we should get moving, Andor," Nicholls said. "We'll check in on you both a bit later in the morning."

"Message if you need anything," Andor said.

"Do you think we're safe out here?"

"For tonight, you are. Tomorrow, they'll want blood. We've managed to put a dent in their plans for now," Nicholls said.

"Do you have enough weapons?" Dex asked.

"We have a trunk full, and the car's parked right outside."

Both men said their goodbyes and headed for their SUV.

Dex closed the cabin door and locked it. He turned to her.

They were alone in the cabin at last. They could finally have some time to catch their breath. Sam was tired, but she'd be up for a repeat of their date night. Her body started to tingle in all the right spots, and her nipples tightened in her bra.

"I'm going to have to have my way with you in every corner of this cabin."

Samantha's skin heated. Her body wanted all of what Dex was offering, and based on his last performance, she knew he would deliver on any promise he made.

He backed her slowly to the couch and started stripping.

She began to shed her clothing too. They were naked in seconds, and he let out a growl. She looked over the expanse of his shoulders and then traced her view all the way down to his hard length. She licked her lips.

He stepped closer and she dropped to her knees. She took him in her mouth, sucking hard. He moaned, and she loved that she was responsible for his pleasure. She licked and sucked and kept her pace up.

"Sam," he moaned.

She sped up, but he pulled her to her feet. "I need to be inside you. Bend over the couch."

She did as he asked.

He slapped her bottom, causing a sharp sting.

She flinched.

"Did I tell you how hard I get when I think of you?"

"No, but I'd like to hear it."

He positioned himself behind her then slowly inched his way into her wetness.

She moaned and her eyes rolled back in her head.

"I get so fucking hard just thinking about you and having you here and scenting your arousal for me, just makes me want to throw you down and have my way with you till you are mindless from pleasure."

Wetness seeped down her thigh. "You are so wet." Dex pumped into her from behind. At first his strokes were a slow torture then he found his pace, and she met every stroke and moan.

Her pleasure was building, and she was ready to erupt. "Dex."

He pumped harder, holding on to her hips.

The sound of their skin slapping together echoed in the cabin.

"Release your pleasure with mine," he groaned out.

"She saw stars and he released his seed in her womb. She was ready to collapse from the sheer pleasure.

Dex kept pumping into her, and another orgasm was building right behind the first. Her moans intensified, and he leaned forward to the juncture of her neck and shoulder while reaching for her nipples. He bit down on her neck and squeezed her nipples, and she erupted. Wave after wave of pleasure crashed through her.

Dex's orgasm was right behind hers. He grunted out as he pumped more of his seed into her soaked pussy.

He pulled out, picked her up in his arms and headed for the bedroom.

"That was... amazing."

"We're only getting started.

Chapter Eighteen

S am had finished showering. She'd taken her time, letting the warm water soothe all the good tingles she was experiencing after a mind-blowing night of passion. She threw on her clothes and followed the scent of coffee and toast to the kitchen.

Dex had everything set out on the table.

She stopped in her tracks and looked at the sexy wolf that was hers. He was dressed and ready for action and even in all that black combat gear he looked scrumptious to her.

"Your look tells me I might have to reconsider my breakfast options." His voice contained that morning huskiness.

She nodded in agreement.

A loud boom outside shook the cabin. Their marginal time in their own paradise had just ended.

Dex grabbed her and pulled her to the bedroom arch. "We need to get outside," he breathed near her ear. "They're going to try to bring this cabin down."

"How did they find us?"

"Let's worry about that later."

"Is there even a way out other than the front door?" She didn't recall a back door.

Her wolf pulled her from the arch, and they staggered to the bedroom. He stuck his hands under the heavy wooden bedframe and toppled it over. On the floor was a trap door. The house shook, and bits of timber started to dislodge. Dex grabbed one of the duffel bags. He bent to pull the trap door open. It flew off the hinges as if it were nothing but paper.

The crash of furniture sounded loudly in her ears. The bedroom was coming apart too, and the wardrobe shook and rattled before it crashed to the floor. Sam dove for Dex's hand, which was out for her to take. He helped her down before lowering himself down too.

The smell of the damp dirt wafted to her nose. She was lying flat on her stomach. It would be a tight crawl.

"Follow me," Dex said.

He had secured the duffel like a backpack to his back and started a slow crawl. Bits of debris fell through the cracks in the wooden flooring.

"It won't hold for much longer. We need to clear this house, now."

They picked up their crawling speed and moved out from under the house seconds before a big fireball hit it. Dex lifted her up and into his arms before sprinting to the dense tree line that was only a foot away. He put her down when he thought they were out of sight.

Her knees wobbled and a soft bubble of laughter escaped her lips. "That was insane."

"That's putting it mildly. They want us dead and will stop at nothing." Dex fished his phone out of his pocket and fired off a text.

"Now let's arm up and get ready to return some fire."

She didn't hesitate. Normally she would never harm a fly, but this lot of bad witches and warlocks had done a good job diminishing any threads of compassion she may have had left in her. Now, she too wanted to inflict damage. "Load me up with everything."

Dex looked up from the duffel bag. He flashed her with a megawatt smile, and her heart did a victory dance. "That's my witch."

He slid a knife in his boot and a pair of special magic disabling cuffs in his cargo pocket. He proceeded to do the same for her. Finally he holstered a gun for her.

"Do you think my magic will work again?"

"It's hard to say, but if it doesn't, we have these weapons."

Shouting could be heard in the distance.

"This is our cue to move," Dex said.

163

"What's the plan?"

"You spray bullets and pray they hit their targets. The faster you slow them down the higher the chance I might be able to slap on a pair of cuffs on one or more."

"What about backup?"

"You and I have each other's backs for at least twenty minutes. That's how long it's going to take Andor and Nicholls to get here."

"What about Lucius?"

"I copied him in. There's no telling how long it will take him. It's always a bonus if he shows up."

"If only we could rely on my power."

"Baby steps, Sam. You did good yesterday."

Her lips dropped. "Only that's not good enough. I need reliability."

"And that will come in due course. Now follow me."

She thought about that power surge from yesterday. It had surprised her as well as that crazy warlock, along with those bat shit crazy witches from her old coven. The look on their faces made every fiber in her rejoice in the best and worst way possible. Best because revenge tasted so sweet on her flaming fingertips and worst because she wanted to inflict as much damage as possible.

Who was she in that instant? Certainly not the defective witch she knew herself to be.

A blast of power flew over their heads.

"Down," Dex shouted.

They dropped at the same time. She could smell the dampness of the foliage. It was still early, and she hadn't even had enough time for coffee. "Those witches are just downright rude."

"That's being nice. I'd like to call them harsher things." Dex motioned for them to crawl deeper into the forest line. Another blast of power hit some trees nearby. One fell.

"Idiots are going to start a fire," Sam said.

"And they haven't one iota of the damage something like that does."

"I'm totally in agreement."

When they had crawled a bit of the way in, Dex stopped and got to his feet before helping her up. He stuck a finger to his lips. She nodded in understanding.

He pulled out a pair of small binoculars and pointed toward the rubble of the cabin. He scanned the area. He took a quick look at his watch. He dropped his voice. "We have to stave them off for another fifteen minutes."

In the situation they were in, crazy magical people on the loose, fifteen minutes was more like eternity. Sam opened her mouth and remembered to keep her volume low. "How are we going to string it out?"

"The old-fashioned way. We're going to play hide and seek for as long as we can. If you were anyone else, I'd say split up, but you're not."

"Dex, I'm okay to divide and conquer." She winked. "I have this baby." She held up the gun he'd given her.

He let out a little chuckle. "While you may be armed and dangerous, I don't trust those witches not to have set up some traps before bringing the house down."

She contemplated what moves they may have made before blowing up the cabin. "You have a point."

"We're stronger together, till reinforcements arrive." He pointed toward the cabin. The witches were stationed around it and looking into the forest for signs of movement. "They'll pounce as soon as we move. On my word, I want you to pick up that rock by your feet and throw it in that direction. I'm going to do the same."

"You think they'll fall for that?" She scrunched up her face. How ridiculous.

A loud bang sounded near the house.

Dex put a finger to his mouth. "No talking after we throw those rocks."

Sam nodded in agreement.

"Now."

They both picked up a rock, tossed it and took off the other way.

As Dex had expected, the witches threw a blast of power toward the rocks. It gave them enough time to move farther into the forest and try to circle back toward the front of the cabin.

They moved slowly, stopping every now and then to let Dex check things out.

They stopped behind a thicket of trees. The driveway to the cabin lay to their left. Dex motioned for her to crouch down. She did as he signaled.

Dex checked his watch again.

"How are we doing?"

"I expect Nicholls and Andor here in approximately two minutes. Prepare for a shit show."

She had figured that once they caught sight of the two men they'd be blasting their power with full force. They watched silently as the witches conversed on what used to be the front porch of the cabin.

The low rumble of a car sounded down the driveway. Dex motioned for them to move. They headed to the halfway point of the long drive that led to the cabin. They stepped out of their cover. A minute later Nicholls and Andor pulled over near them and exited the vehicle.

"I hope you brought enough ammo," Dex said.

Andor gave him a toothy grin. "Like you need to ask."

"Sam. You okay?" Nicholls asked.

"I'd be better without those menacing witches and warlocks." No sooner had she said the words than a ball of magic came charging past them.

They'd been discovered.

Blasts of power hit near them. Both Nicholls and Andor sped for cover, and Sam had little time to process because strong hands lifted her over a sturdy shoulder and the world turned upside down. Dex was running for the thicket of trees. She heard shouts and guns going off and knew in her over-the-shoulder position Nicholls and Andor were firing at the witches.

Dex put her down. Andor circled around the other side.

Another blast of power hit some nearby trees, and Sam was grateful the witches couldn't accurately hit targets.

"This might be quicker in wolf form."

"I think we need a combo attack," Dex said. "You and Andor shift. I'll stay with Sam."

Sam watched as both men started to unbuckle their gear. "Whoa." She turned her head and Dex stepped in front of her, a low growl emitting from his lips. He was jealous of her seeing other men. Her lips tugged at the corners. After mating with Dex there would never be another for either of them, and she liked it that way.

"Okay, you can turn," Dex informed.

She turned her head and both men were in wolf form. Andor was a dark brown with reddish streaks and Nicholls was a dark blond. They let out a growl and took off into the forest.

Dex turned and pointed toward the witches. Then fired a round of shots. He got one in the leg.

The other two took off in the other direction, leaving a very stunned witch on the ground. "We've only got a few moments before she regains her power.

Dex and Samantha moved to where the witch squealed in pain. Blood seeped from her leg, but at least she couldn't use any magic. Dex slapped a pair of cuffs around her wrists.

"You'll pay for this."

"How about we worry about who will pay for what when you're in front of the high witches' counsel. But if you pester me, I'll just hand you over to the vampire, Xen Lyson, and let his *Phi Athanatoi* decide what kind of punishment should be met."

The wounded witch's eyes went wide, and she paled at Dex's words.

Dex unbuckled a medical unit and proceeded to patch her up. "This should stem the blood for the time being." He lifted her with ease and pushed her toward Nicholls and Andor's SUV. Dex secured her inside and turned to Sam.

"Where do you think the other two witches got to?"

"They can't have gone far. Nicholls and Andor will already be in position," Dex said. "Come on." He steered them back into the bushes so they could make their way up to the house without being detected.

They were careful not to make a sound. When they got close to the house, they found the witches huddled over something, chanting.

"Whatever incantation they're using..." a rock formed in Samantha's stomach "... it isn't good."

"They're calling for backup."

"We'll be outnumbered. We can't take them all, Dex."

"Then we need to attack before they succeed in getting that mayday call out."

Dex let out a low growl. She heard it only because of her proximity.

"Stay here," he said.

Several things played out in slow-mo straight after that.

Nicholls and Andor both bolted from their hiding spots toward the witches. Dex did the same. Blasts of power flew toward Dex. He ducked and weaved. Andor and Nicholls cornered the other witches.

Samantha took in the scene before her. They were there for her. She couldn't sit like some stuffed pigeon and watch. No, she knew she had to be a part of the action. She stepped out of the thick shrubbery and headed straight for all the mayhem.

Chapter Nineteen

"Duck," Dex shouted.

That she could do without anything defective happening. She dropped low as a blast of fiery power headed her way. These witches were nasty. If only she could rely on her power, she'd zap their asses to Siberia. She came up behind Dex.

"Stay there. When I say fire, take out the gun and plug these bitches."

"Ready when you are."

Dex stuck his fingers in his mouth. His whistle sounded loud and clear.

Samantha kept her eyes on the witches and saw the exact moment when Andor and Nicholls attacked. All hell broke loose. The witches stopped their chant and threw power blasts at both wolves. It sent them flying backward. They hit the ground—hard.

"Now," Dex shouted and Samantha released random shots. Spray-and-pray was definitely the strategic approach. She moved in the direction of the witches, firing, and hoping she hit something. They threw power toward her. She twitched her nose and hoped it would work.

The speeding power balls changed direction and went up in the air then started to fall back to earth, propelling themselves toward the witches. They were both chanting. It appeared they would be hit by their own power. Samantha high-fived herself internally.

The witches were throwing power toward Dex, and he weaved left and right to avoid anything they threw. Andor and Nicholls had recovered and raced back in. The air shifted and Samantha realized something else was coming.

A blast of power hit, and Ben was back but with an entourage. One decimated the power heading for the witches, and Ben threw a blast of power that tossed them all backward and onto the hard ground.

Samantha heard a crack and searing pain traveled down her leg. "Argh." She let out a loud moan. They were doomed. Blasts of power were directed at them, and Samantha twitched her nose, but nothing happened. Where the hell was Lucius? They needed him. There was no way they would defeat Ben and the fresh batch of witches and warlocks.

Dex must have shifted because he made his way to her in his wolf form. She looked into his eyes and heard clear as day, *Call the warlock*, in her mind.

She closed her eyes and whispered, "Lucius."

The seconds ticked by, and Ben threw a wave of power.

Dex put his paws over Sam to protect her. A flash of light stung her eyes. She was sure they'd been obliterated, and she floated in some space of white brilliance. It was so bright she closed her eyes.

A wolf howl sounded in her ears—Dex. She could feel him still covering her. They weren't dead. She opened her eyes to see Lucius a few feet away, firing power back in Ben's direction, but he had help too. It looked like members of the high court. She didn't know them by name, but she did know some of their faces.

Lucius made his way to her. "How badly are you hurt?"

"I think I've broken a bone or something in my leg."

Dex moved his huge weight from her.

Lucius quickly examined her left leg, touching the area from her knee down. She winced when his fingers brushed the troubled spot near her ankle. "It's definitely broken. I can feel the swelling."

"Dex, I'm going to need you in human form. Try to get Sam to the car. We'll do as much as we can."

Dex trotted off into the forest to where they'd been watching the witches.

The two wolves Andor and Nicholls came over to her.

Lucius got up. "I have to rejoin the fight."

Andor and Nicholls let out a growl.

Samantha slowly tried to sit up.

Andor put a paw on her.

"I want to see what's going on."

Dex emerged from the forest line, armed to the teeth. He made his way to her in a flash. He moved fast even in human form.

He looked at Andor and Nicholls. "I'll need one of you to shift back."

The wolves looked at each other, and Nicholls took off to where they'd shed their clothes and gear.

A few seconds later Nicholls emerged armed and ready. Blasts of power flew in every direction. Team Lucius was gaining the upper hand.

"Sam, I'm taking you to the car." Dex put his hands under her and lifted her carefully.

Pain shot up her leg, and she let out a scream.

"It's okay, baby, we'll get this fixed."

She knew Dex could feel her pain too and all her crazy emotions.

"I need to bury this guy." Dex's anger pulsed through his words.

"Do your thing." He kissed her and turned back in the direction of all the chaos.

Dex had had enough.

"Nicholls, Ander. Work on surrounding Ben, and let Lucius and his witches and warlocks fight the others. It's the only chance we have."

They nodded and took off.

He did the same. He took off back into the forest and came to a spot where he could see Ben clearly. He wanted nothing more than to shift and go for the jugular, but he couldn't do that. He knew the head of the coven wanted Ben alive so they could deliver their own punishment. Dex would honor it.

A few blasts of power made Ben stumble. Dex took that opportunity to fire bullets. He filled Ben with two magazines of bullets. Ben waved an arm to throw power at him, but it no longer worked. Dex pulled out his cuffs and smacked them in place. The crew Ben had collected for this fight disappeared when they saw their ringleader captured.

"You are all vermin."

"I think you've got that the other way around."

Ben scoffed. "You know nothing."

"I know your death will be slow," Dex promised.

Chapter Twenty

The bell on the shop door tingled and her sexy hot neighbor walked in with a huge smile on his face. He winked at her.

She was ogling and had every right to. He was hers. He pulled the bouquet she had in her hands from her and placed it on the counter. Then he pulled her in for a hot searing kiss. After a few moments of panty melting bliss, she came up for air. "Dex, I'm working."

"I know and I'll only be a minute. I just wanted to stop in and give you something before heading to my meeting."

He was going to meet with his previous employer who was in town.

The bell sounded again. Samantha's breath caught and her mouth went dry and clammy. In walked a tall man with a presence that both warned and enthralled those in the room. He was smiling in their direction.

Dex's head whipped around. "Boss."

The man closed the distance quickly and stuck out his hand for Dex. They shook hands and then gave each other a hug and pat on the back.

"I was just making my way to our meeting," Dex said.

"I was early. I thought I'd come and find you."

Sam watched with interest. The man held a folder in his left hand.

"This is Samantha, my mate," Dex said.

Sam stuck out her hand and hobbled over.

"Meet Xen. The head of the organization I used to work for," Dex introduced.

Xen's hand closed around hers and an instant calm washed over her. "Lovely to meet you, Samantha."

Her heart sped up and she got dragged into his orbit of a smile. There was something dazzling about the man. Dex growled beside her.

"Relax, wolf. I'm spoken for." He dropped Sam's hand. "I thought Samantha might want this." He handed her the file.

"What is it?"

"A collected history of your family from our database."

Her mouth opened. Then closed. "How?"

"My organization has spent many years collecting information for our database. Any supernatural creatures or beings are added to the system, and we keep a close eye on things. It helps maintain a quiet existence alongside humans."

Samantha mulled over what Xen divulged. "Isn't that an invasion of privacy. Knowing and keeping tabs on people?"

"Trust me when I say we never invade anyone's privacy unless the need arises. Your coven has been the subject of a few investigations over the years. There have been witches who've been brought before the witches and warlocks' council. I hadn't realized the severity of their corruption till Dex called me."

"What will happen?"

"In short, there will be a mass reshuffle amongst the current covens. I can't intervene with what goes on there."

Sam thought about that for a moment. "If you had stepped in sooner, perhaps..."

Xen lifted his hand. "We didn't know the extent of the corruption until you fought with Ben. At that point Dex had decided to take him on."

She fell silent for a moment. Processing.

"I guess we aren't any closer to knowing why he wanted to kill me. It seems he hated my parents.

"There may be some answers in that file." Xen pointed to the folder in her hands. He turned to Dex. "Do you need time?"

"I'll catch up with you in a minute," Dex replied.

Xen turned to Samantha again and stuck out his hand. "A pleasure to meet you."

She giggled. He was dazzling in a way she couldn't describe. "Thank you for this."

He let her hand go and exited the shop, oozing power and grace.

"That man, what is he?"

"A lethal vampire."

Samantha stared at the spot where he'd been. "Funny, he doesn't come across like that."

"That's what makes him dangerous."

Her chest tightened. Her world had turned on its head. Nothing would ever be the same. All these creatures she had only heard about were now around her.

"Will you be okay if I leave you for a while? I need to brief Xen on what happened at the cabin."

"Sure, I'm just going to sit over by the counter and read what's in here." She patted the folder with one hand.

"Okay. I'll read over it later."

"Go to your meeting. You'll be late." She shooed him with one hand. On the inside she was bursting to start reading the contents of the file.

Dex reached for her and pulled her to him. "I know you're curious about what's in there." He dropped his glance to the folder that now sat squashed between the two of them.

"I know you're very interested in what I may find in there.

"You think?" He chuckled. Then dropped his mouth to hers.

She moaned and he deepened the kiss. It was clear what he wanted—her.

He broke the kiss. "Any thoughts you have, hold them till tonight."

Every time he kissed her, he left her boneless.

"How about I help you over to the counter so you can sit on the stool."

She nodded. He proceeded to settle her with the file in front of her.

"I'll see you in a few minutes. This shouldn't take long." Dex walked toward the entrance.

Sam flipped the cover open. It only took a moment for her grey matter to realize the depth of what she was looking at. The file wasn't just about her and her parents; it was also about her grandparents and aunts and uncles. She hadn't thought she had anyone after her parents disappeared. The file made her both happy and sad. Sad that no one came forward from either family to claim her and take her in as their own. And happy because as she scanned through more documents she learned the magic in her family came from an old line of witches that could be traced back seven hundred years.

"Wow."

She leafed through more pages. There were photographs along with biographies of each family member. Thick tears welled in her eyes. One made a slow trail down her cheek. It brought her joy to look upon these witches and wizards. They were her family. Family she didn't know and family she wanted to connect with.

She turned over more pages. Each page in the file gave her added insight. She was surprised to find some of her magical relatives lived overseas. She came to a few pages about her parents and some news articles on things they'd done for their magical community. They seemed like decent people. Why did Ben hate them so much?

She turned to another page that showed school photos of her parents, Lucius and even Ben. Nothing looked out of the ordinary until she spotted a headline from the witches' council. "Competition for older witch and warlock families. Winner gets unlimited access to magical library."

She saw her mother had won, and beside her was Ben with a sour look on his face.

"All this over a competition for library access?"

The bell on the shop tingled and Dex walked in, followed by two customers.

He walked over to her and glanced down at the open folder.

One of the ladies who entered the shop picked a bunch of ready-to-go bouquets that Jack had helped put together for quick sales. They were going to go with this for the next few weeks until her leg healed. She helped the customer and processed her payment. When they were out of the shop, she turned to Dex.

He stared at something in concentration.

"What is it?"

He pointed to the page. "Think this has a lot to do with everything."

It was her family tree, and it didn't just go back 700 years.

It went back farther to the mid 9th century B.C.

"That's impossible." She gasped.

"It's not. Xen is older than that."

Sam dropped her weight on the stool.

"Do you think that's what Ben meant when he said my line is vermin and should be extinguished?"

"I'd say so."

"Still, that shouldn't be reason enough for hate."

"No, but..." Dex shuffled a few of the papers "... this says a lot. He wanted access to the library and didn't win. Your mother did. He was jealous."

"All for library access?"

Dex shifted to look at her. "No, Sam. This is like the key to the kingdom for magical folks. They'd have access to the council's popular spells but also to much older not practised spells."

"You mean like dark magic."

"Exactly."

"All this was because Ben wanted what he couldn't get to, but it's still not a solid enough reason to target my parents or me."

"Read this." Dex flipped over a few pages and stabbed a finger at one.

"The year your parents went missing there was going to be another competition. There are four old families in these parts. Your mother had won for several years because the other two weren't that great, but Ben was up there with your mother. He wanted to remove his competition so he could win."

"But I'm no competition. My magic is defective."

"Doesn't matter. To him you were your mother's child and still a threat that could one day see him barred from his access."

"Power," Sam whispered.

"Yes, it's always about power."

She started gathering the papers together to put back in the file.

"How about we go through everything tonight. I'll pick you up and we'll grab a bite to eat first."

"That sounds..." Samantha didn't finish her sentence because Lucius materialized.

"The council has bound Ben's powers."

"That will make him crazy, won't it?" Sam asked.

"Given his actions, it's a fair punishment."

A pang of sadness hit her in the chest.

"Don't feel sorry for him. He would kill you if he were given that chance again."

"You're right."

"It's not the only reason I'm here."

A rock dropped in her belly. She couldn't take any more bad news.

"We have a lead as to where your parents might be."

"What, they're alive?" She shot to her feet and pain stabbed her in the leg. She'd forgotten.

Dex grabbed her and helped her back to the stool. "Stay there."

She looked back at Lucius, who looked pleased. "I've never stopped looking."

"I'm helping no matter what," Sam said.

"Warlock, you're not doing this alone," Dex added.

"How soon can you pack?"

Thank You

Thank you for reading *One Wolf Next Door*! I truly appreciate your support and hope you had fun reading it. I had a blast writing it, and it was meant to be a breezy and entertaining escape.

If you enjoyed it, I would be grateful if you could leave a review on your favourite retailer's platform. Reviews are the lifeblood of our work. They help other readers discover books like this one and keep the magic alive.

Thank you again for being part of Samantha's and Dex's journey.

Next in The Willow Witch Chronicles

READ A SHORT EXCERPT BELOW.

Read an excerpt below.

ONE

S amantha Willow's once quiet life in Bel Haven had
turned from normal to a whole new level of drama. Mr
Rutherford, a customer and a frequent one at that, had turned
up dead as a doornail in front of Bewitching Blooms–her shop.

The events that followed cascaded into an all-out battle
between her and a coven that wanted her dead. The nerve,
thinking they could just wipe her out for no reason other
than that they believed she hailed from a long line of powerful
witches.

"As if I have that kind of arsenal up my sleeve," she huffed.

Fortunately, or unfortunately, it skipped her. Her power, if
she could call it that, was as potent as the steam on a cup of
coffee. A mere wisp of nothingness.

"And what is it with witches and competitions?" She
queried, looking down at Gilbert while she threw some
underwear into her luggage.

Gilbert barked back a few times, then got up from where he
was sitting and pushed on his hind legs. He put his paws on her
suitcase and barked again.

She swore that if he could talk, he would. "I'd be happy to zap
someone's ass whenever I wanted to, instead of only when my
stupid power decided to show up."

A heavy sigh escaped her lips. Her magic was the bane of her
existence and the reason she had been cast out. Still, deep down

in the pit of her stomach, she knew she had more to give. If only they had given her the chance and trained her properly.

Gilbert released two more barks.

"True, I am a bit better than I was before." At her words, he resumed his position on the floor while she threw in another pair of jeans and closed the suitcase, moving it to the floor before she pulled the handle up so she could wheel it to the stairs. Gilbert sprinted out the door before her and was at the bottom of the staircase, looking up and barking.

"I can get a simple suitcase down the stairs, Gilbert. Shush."

Samantha didn't get to try. The bag disappeared from her hand and appeared at the bottom of the stairs. Standing next to it was Lucius.

"You know I could have taken care of that myself."

"I don't doubt it, but why make life difficult?"

Sam turned up her nose as she made her way down. "Wise ass." A small smile tugged at her lips. His powerful magic had helped heal her fractured ankle.

"You haven't practised any spells for days."

She scoffed. "Like I've had a chance." It took her a second, then she whipped her head up and met his gaze. "How do you know what I have and haven't done?"

Lucius' lips curled up into a smile. "I know things."

"I don't need you spying on me."

The doorbell rang.

Gilbert, who had been awfully quiet for a few seconds, started barking.

Lucius waved his hand, and the door opened.

"You know you could take a step and use your hands."

"Too much effort." Lucius grinned.

Gilbert was already on his hind legs and glued to Dex's leg.

"Who's got surveillance on you?" he asked, shifting his duffel bag to pet her crazy dog.

She threw a thumb gesture in Lucius' direction. "He does."

"Warlock, why are you watching my mate?"

"I'm not watching her *per se*. Just a tiny spell to let me know if she's practising."

Dex stepped into her space and pulled her close. His eyebrows knitted. "You haven't been twitching your nose, have you?"

"I've been busy."

He dropped a soft kiss to her lips and released her. "If you don't do as instructed, you'll lose the power you have strived to get a handle on."

"Let's see what my power does." She twitched her nose, and the suitcase shot up to the ceiling, stayed suspended for several seconds before flying straight at her and Dex.

Dex pulled her into an embrace and turned them around so he could absorb the impact.

*** End of Sample ***

To continue reading Two Times The Curse, pick up a copy at your favourite retailer!

ABOUT THE AUTHOR

EFTHALIA IS AN AUSTRALIAN AUTHOR WHO WRITES FANTASY PARANORMAL ROMANCE, INSPIRED BY HER LOVE OF GREEK MYTHOLOGY.

HER FASCINATION WITH STORYTELLING BEGAN WITH THE STORIES HER MOTHER SHARED DURING HER CHILDHOOD, SPARKING HER INTEREST IN FANTASY WORLDS. SHE LOVES NOTHING MORE THAN GETTING LOST IN THE WORLD OF GREEK GODS, DROOL WORTHY VAMPIRES, AND KNOCK YOUR SOCKS OFF WEREWOLVES WHO RISK EVERYTHING FOR FEISTY AND COURAGEOUS HEROINES.

FOR MORE INFORMATION:
WEBSITE: HTTPS://WWW.EFTHALIAAUTHOR.COM
NEWSLETTER SIGN-UP:
HTTPS://WWW.EFTHALIAAUTHOR.COM/NEWSLETTER/
E-MAIL: EFTHALIA@EFTHALIAAUTHOR.COM

Also by Efthalia

PHI ATHANATOI SERIES
Phantasma: The Awakening
Phantasia: A Bad Day on Olympus
Phoenix: The Rise

THE WILLOW WITCH CHRONICLES
One Wolf Next Door
Two Times the Curse

ANTHOLOGY SHORT STORIES
Bewitched Warrior Cats (Hellcats Anthology)
Kerberos (Hellhounds Anthology)
Crimson Crown (Rotten to the Core Anthology)

NOVELLA
Tattoo (A Phi Athanatoi Short)

www.ingramcontent.com/pod-product-compliance
Lightning Source LLC
Chambersburg PA
CBHW020009140726
47904CB00018B/2136